AN
EXTRA KNOT

A Different World War
(PART II)

HUGH LUPUS

An Extra Knot (Part II) ©2019 APS Publications
All rights reserved.

A catalogue record for this book is available from the British Library

ISBN 9781789960198

APS Publications,
4 Oakleigh Road,
Stourbridge,
West Midlands,
DY8 2JX

www.andrewsparke.com

PUSH

It had been a good season Jorge thought. The invasion of his homeland had bogged down in a swamp of bitter enmity. Wherever the Fascists went they found enemies. Man, woman or child it did not matter, everyone was an enemy. Kill and butcher as they might that enmity never faltered, never ended.

Burnt houses sheltered them, burnt fields fed them.

For them there was no respite, no rest. Sentries nervous when on duty were found dead when relieved. Men and women, armed only with courage and explosives ran forward immolating themselves on men, tanks and artillery.

He no longer led an army but a people. A war fought on their behalf had become their war, their cause. Their blood had become an unquenchable votive.

And now at long last the trickle of supplies from France had widened. It was not a raging torrent, for France still fought Germany in a curiously quiet war. But it was enough.

It was no longer time to defend. It was time to attack.

Now while the world's eyes gazed upon other scenes.

Now in winter's cold as the last of the old year died.

He had called together his lieutenants. El Platero with his scarred face, Alvarez with his poetry and O'Neil of the cold eyes. Together they studied maps, listened to the reports of spies, heard from the government in Gijón and at last asked but two questions.

Where was the enemy weakest? And would attacking him there aid them?

At last conscience as much as strategy dictated the answer. The Basques had been attacked, had fought with dauntless courage and even now resisted those who still held the fairer parts of those lands they claimed for their own. The Fascists had retreated but not far enough. It was time to turn east towards the rising sun.

It was time to free the Basques.

It was a thin soup, perhaps a single potato had gone into the making of it but it was doubly warming. It had the normal warming effect any soup will have on a cold winters morning but warmer still was the fact that he suspected that it was the last food that the peasant family had. The old grandmother had stood before him, grave and dignified with the steaming bowl before her. The act was both gracious and deeply troubling.

To accept would be to take food from the two children who sat watching him with wide eyes from the corner of the room.

There were no parents in this family, like many others they had vanished, lost in the mass arrests that followed the collapse of Basque resistance in this part of the country. There was only the old grandmother who had stood before him, grey faced and trembling with suppressed hunger.

Jorge took the bowl and drank deeply from it expressing his thanks with stumbling heartfelt words, vowing that he would ensure that this family at least would not starve. The bowl was still more than half full; he beckoned the two children over and they eagerly drank the remainder.

He looked over towards the grandmother who nodded her thanks. Her honour and the honour of her house had been satisfied and her guest had been fed. There was no more to be said and he rubbed the sleep out of his eyes and turned to his maps.

There wasn't much left of the town and it was but a small stopping place on his drive east but he had no choice other than to liberate it.

Others had come to him, begging that this place above all others should be liberated. He had argued that his route lay further south but they argued that their heart should be free and that without that heart they were but half a people. They had brought letters from his government in Gijón and pleas from exiles across the world.

He had grumbled, complaining about interference, knowing that to advance here would stretch his limited resources but had at last agreed.

His calloused fingers traced lines on the map. His advances, possible counter moves, responses to those moves, reserves, regiments and artillery; all made a single picture in his mind.

Outside there was a rumble of guns.

The battle for Guernica had begun.

He was a long way from home.

A long way from barnstorming over dusty Mid-West towns.

A long way from a tattered newspaper that told of an exciting life as a volunteer in the Asturian Air Force.

A long way from home.

He shivered with cold. The snow clouds had vanished and taken their illusion of warmth with them. The air was a cold demon that tore at him with claws of adamantine ice and distorted his face into a permanent grimace.

His old Dewoitine no longer fought impossible battles with other, better fighters. Now it had other duties. Four bombs hung from his aircraft and though they were not large, they had the seeds of many deaths within them. Today newer fighters would protect him while he sowed those seeds.

Even now as his squadron sped forward they were twisting, turning and dying above him.

The earth below was a patchwork of churned mud and fresh snow. He could see the guns below him open fire and moments later the shells reach their targets. This was his signal.

Without looking to see if he was being followed he pushed his craft down and the ground rose up to meet him.

Faster and faster. Nearer and nearer.

Tiny puffs of black cloud attempted to claw him from the air but he felt invulnerable. His job today was to kill the protecting infantry, separate them from the tanks and guns leaving both unguarded and vulnerable.

He could see faces now, mere blobs, pale in the winter sunshine. And that was close enough. A quick burst of machine gun fire and his bombs burst amongst the white blobs.

The ground reached out for him in a deadly embrace but he soared away no longer cold but strangely warm.

It was time to fly home.

This was war as Georges Seurat remembered it.

Now there was no more hiding in caves or isolated farmhouses venturing out to kill and scurry away. Now he was in the open with his old friend beside him. To his left and to his right were other French exiles and their seventy fives. And beyond them were other guns large and small, each one brought with much labour and no small amount of blood to this place and this time. Each one pointed towards the enemy, each one was eager to spread death to the enemy.

Behind him lay the infantry who hoped that this day they would pour unharmed through the single gap that Georges would provide.

He took a long swallow from the bottle of rough wine which never left his side and grimaced at the bitter acidic taste. Wine was wine, that was true but even he had standards and this wine fell far below what was an acceptable vintage. He thought again of his homeland and its wines. When war had broken out, he had thought of returning home but what use would his country have for a broken artilleryman more than half in love with the bottle?

So he had stayed, determined to show that despite red rimmed eyes he could still shoot as well as ever.

He looked up and far above him another battle was taking place. Small insects each one the temporary home of a man turned in circles or fell trailing smoke. He could do nothing to help them. His world was here in the mud and the cold.

There was a sharp order and he pulled the lanyard that allowed his gun to vomit death. All around him other guns did the same in a staggered, barking roar. He ignored them as he fell into the familiar pattern of reloading.

France may no longer want him but Spain needed him. It was a comforting thought.

And one day, perhaps soon, he would become used to Spanish wine.

In Guernica the buildings sat like ruined teeth.

Without windows, without doors, capped not with roofs but with charred beams and flame smashed stones. They had absorbed much these fractured houses. They had seen pain and blood and loss. They had covered the dead with their fabric like a solid shroud. They had stood proud while lies had been heaped upon them. They were the keepers of memories.

Memories old.

Memories new.

Memories of conquerors with swagger who gazed with imperial gaze. Memories of these victors going out to battle with those who came to free. Memories of beaten men swarming to safety.

In Guernica the buildings sat like ruined teeth.

And they had been delivered.

All things considered it was a remarkable service. The Mass, despite being in the open air was the same as it had always been. But the fact that it was being celebrated at all was sufficient cause for joy. Though the man at the makeshift altar looked less than happy, and perhaps that was not too surprising, most men who had received such a beating would have good cause to show such a sorrowful face.

Not that it mattered what the Bishop thought. After all he was, as far as Jorge was concerned, living on borrowed time. The man and a suitcase full of vestments and church property had been found attempting to flee after the Fall of Guernica.

Unfortunately for him it was Jorge's men who found him and even more unfortunately recognised him. Only the arrival of a band of Basque irregulars saved him and he bought his life with the promise of support and prayers.

It was the one great difference between his forces and the people he was now allied with. Despite many slights and insults the Basques had remained firmly wedded to their religion and refused to give it up. For Jorge and most of the Asturians the Church was an instrument of oppression and one they would gladly eradicate.

Which is why attending today's mass was so hard.

And so necessary.

He needed the Basques almost as much as they needed him and his army. Without them, without their aid, his march to the French border would be that much harder.

To fight in the midst of a sea of friends where the enemy drowned under the weight of ten thousand drops of hate was one thing but to fight here where emotions and thoughts were subtly different was another.

He needed French supplies, French supplies that did not have to be carried over disputed mountain passes, through half held towns, through lands that the Basques had held even as most of their lands fell to the Fascists. Without supplies, without secure routes, the brightening flame of Basque resistance would dim once more and even his own land would be in danger.

So today he stood under grey skies, in front of the shell-scarred stump of an ancient tree and listened while a man that he would see dead chanted the half-forgotten words of the mass and he mouthed words that he had sworn would never fill his mouth again.

All in the cause of friendship.

After an eternity of gritted teeth the mass ended and the area in front of the tree was cleared. Two small boys carried a wooden plaque and placed it in front of the tree before turning to read the words that had been carved into it. The thin voices of the boys did not carry far but that was not important; it was the declaration cut into the salvaged and charred wood that was important.

The boys had obviously practised hard because they did not once hesitate or falter.

'This is our tree.

This is a Basque tree.

This is where our freedom was born, this is where it died and this is where it has been given new life.

This is where we pledge before all that we will not cease to fight until the roots of our tree rest in free soil.

This we swear.'

Jorge thought they were fine words, though he was no judge and certainly no scholar. He was what he was. He was what circumstances had forced him to become. A general and a leader of men.

So the only question in his mind was whether the fine words, would be translated into action.

Could he rely on the Basques to feed not only their own men but his? Could he rely on them to keep open the thin, wavering supply lines that kept both alive? Could he rely on them to put their common interests before all others?

They were questions he could not answer. He was at heart a simple man who felt most comfortable on the battlefield.

The questions would have to wait; others could answer him, if they could catch him. Because by the days end he intended that his eyes would be looking not at crowds of excited people but at the road that led east. He could not go too far wrong if he placed his army before the enemy and the sooner he did that the better.

A campaign in summer hills and summer valleys would bring him to the border and a France who would surely welcome an ally while she fought Germany on the roads which led to the Rhine.

It was a good plan, a sensible plan

And a long road to the border.

Georges Seurat had wept tears without number.

They all had.

Not a single tear changed what had happened.

They had drunk the rough Spanish wine until their stomachs rebelled. Each bottle was sacrificed in vain. France, their France, their own land had fallen. They were lost, marooned and adrift with no hope of succour.

A thousand mad schemes were proposed and rejected, and when the last tear had dried and the last bottle had been drunk they were left with but one option.

Fight on.

Fight on, as much for their own lost land as for the Asturians and Basques who fought with them. Fight on. For hate. For pride.

France in a last despairing act had given up her hoarded treasure and for a brief, mad few weeks the trickle of supplies had turned into a raging torrent.

Georges had taken that torrent and turned it into a deadly river of hate. His gun was never silent and each round was in his mind not sent by him alone but by a still defiant and vengeful France. There was no thought of halting now, no thought of consolidating, of following any other path but that of war. The Fascists appeared before him and he destroyed them seeing them not as men but as beasts, despoilers of his own land.

A whole army felt as he did; to slacken now would be to suffer a horrid fate, their security lay only through the dead bodies of their enemy. And so they pushed.

They pushed east towards a now exhausted France and south through an enemy who had come to expect defeat.

They pushed hard. Every day they killed and were killed. And each death spurred Georges on to push a little longer and a little harder.

Until one morning he woke to see the morning sun shining pinkly on the Pyrenees.

SWORDS

The irony was not lost on Leon Blum as he drove through the rain to await an uncertain future. He had built a coalition out of division and envy and those very forces were combining against him. He had taught France that she could act as one, speak as one. And so she had, though the acts were not all that he wished and the voice was less than strident. But he had done something to be proud of, something that the history books would speak of in the years to come.

Or so he hoped.

The future was always uncertain, though he could guess his own future with certainty. The losses at Sedan were the trigger to the start of his downfall of him and his government

An anxious Churchill flew to see him with questions, suggestions and proposals. None of those halted the German advance.

Not for a single minute.

Paris was lost and they retreated and the political divisions that had riven France for decades travelled with them. But German hammer blows had welded some divisions into an alloy. And a strange alloy it was; though mostly hard right it had elements of pacifism and those whose only god was Moscow. A new sword had been forged and though blunt it was enough to defeat him.

A government was being born. Born with only one aim. To seek peace with a victorious Germany. France would seek peace. A despairing, submissive peace but she would lay down her sword.

Although there were others who would gladly fight on and it was to them he now looked. He still had power. For a few more hours he could still give orders, and in the confusion that the next few weeks would bring there would be none to gainsay them.

He would open the gates of French arsenals. Every warehouse would empty, every camp would close, every boot, bullet and cannon would be sent south. The Asturians would have all the swords they could use.

Leon Blum Prime Minister, socialist, politician and failed healer of France walked into his hotel room and sat down onto the hard bed, eyes half closed in fatigue. He had not achieved victory but as a man he had not been defeated. He had fought against a great evil. He had fought to the very end.

And as a last defiant act he had upheld the honour of France.

Who was he?

The ditch was safe but it was cold and damp and successfully beat back any of his attempts to sleep. So he stared up at the sky and watched the stars whizz past the sluggish clouds.

So who was he?

Was he Matthew Dodd, ambitious articled clerk at Sharp and Harper?

Or was he Sergeant Dodd, part time soldier, the son and grandson of a long line of Rifle Brigade soldiers.

Was he the man who loved the detail and ambiguity of the law or the man who loved the hard edged absolutes that came with wearing the uniform?

He could not decide.

The stars gave him no answer and the clouds whispered only nonsense.

Perhaps it would be better to decide what he wasn't. He certainly was not the man in the immaculate uniform who stepped off the boat at Bordeaux all those months ago mind filled with parade ground theory. No, that man was dead, very dead; had died in fact only a few days after he had heard rifles crack in real anger.

He'd been taught hard lessons, by hard teachers and he had seen what had happened to those who failed to learn. So that made him a soldier, at least for now and, if it was not too flattering a word to use of himself, a veteran.

And an outcast, though perhaps a lucky one. Cut off from his unit and unable to return, he had wandered, some inner demon denying him even the thought of surrender. Convinced that salvation lay forever in the next valley, he had wandered south, stealing from farmhouses and fields, sleeping in barns if he was lucky or like tonight in an unfriendly ditch. And tonight as he had done many nights before he promised himself that tomorrow he would be delivered from his troubles and his journey would end.

Sleep, though fitful at last claimed him and then released him to the pre-dawn half-light and he began again his journey south. All that he owned was with him, and it took but a moment to gather up his belongings and stretch his legs south.

He avoided roads. Roads were dangerous; they held cars and people so he avoided them, crossing them only whenever there was no choice.

And this morning he had no choice.

He felt safe enough now; the road was narrow, barely big enough for two cars to pass with ease. And the sun had barely begun to rise. The world was still a mixture of half light and dark pools of shadow. And that was how he nearly missed the car.

It stood black, painted in black shadow and beside it stood a collection of darkness that might just be a man. He cursed his lack of vision and dropped to the ground, rifle pointing resolutely towards the car. The sun rose and as it rose his finger tightened on the trigger.

If he attempted to continue his journey now the man would see him and possibly betray him.

The man made a half-hearted and futile attempt to start the car and then sat on the cold road, head in his hands, exuding great waves of despair and sadness. Even Matthew, a man who prided himself on his self-sufficiency, felt the wave of despair wash over him and an answering wave of empathy flood within him.

The man was obviously alone, just as he was.

His finger relaxed on the trigger and he stood up, rising out of the vanishing darkness. The man jumped and ran behind the car, placing it between him and Matthew.

Matthew shouted out that he would not shoot in what he thought was passable French. There was a wry chuckle and the man walked slowly from around the car, hands held by his sides.

'Your grammar is terrible, and your accent leaves much to be desired.' The man spoke in perfect English with only a ghost of a French accent. 'Permit me to introduce myself, I am Georges Mandel and until a short time ago I had the honour to be a Minister in the government of France,' he smiled bitterly. 'But now I am but a leaf blown by the wind. Yet within me you see not a man but a small flame and I hope that my flame will yet burn brighter.' He gestured towards his car. 'I had an appointment but first my driver abandoned me and then my car decided that it would move no more.'

Matthew explained just how he been cut off from his company and had wandered south ever since as the coast roads and routes east were full of refugees and German patrols.

Mandel looked a little upset on receiving the news that escape to the west was now an impossibility and then looked shrewdly at the sergeant. The look solidified an idea which had been forming in Matthew's mind and he almost unwillingly gave voice to it. 'Best you come with me then, sir. There's no hope of you getting out otherwise.' A thought struck him. 'Unless, that is, you want to surrender.'

Mandel vigorously shook his head and Matthew grinned at the sight.

'That's settled then sir.' He looked down at his companions' feet. 'Best we find you some boots before too long then.'

Mandel returned the grin. 'And which way is south sergeant?'

'That way sir.'

Mandel gave a last look at his once shiny car and began to stride in the direction that Matthew had pointed. 'Under the circumstances,' he said, 'It would be best if you call me Georges.'

The boots were stolen from a farmhouse many days and many kilometres away but they no longer rubbed and he had adapted his walk to copy that of his companion. Georges Mandel had noticed that Matthew's eyes were never still and his hand never let go of his rifle. It was strangely comforting to have Dodd as a companion. He felt safer having him by his side.

They were thieves.

No farm house, no isolated village, no unattended car was safe from their attentions, though Mandel insisted, much to Dodd's amusement on leaving promissory notes payable upon a government no longer in existence.

'I am not a thief Matthew,' he explained unconvincingly. 'We are merely borrowing these things and one day I will repay every centime.'

Dodd had laughed at him but he had explained that this was merely a temporary situation and as a former minister of the French Republic he could not descend to burglary. Dodd had continued to laugh but deep inside had been left feeling foolish.

They had exchanged stories about very different lives.

Dodd was the son and grandson of soldiers, growing up in the back streets of a provincial city, and through what Mandel could only imagine was a great deal of determination and hard work he had gained a scholarship to a school which offered more than a basic education and from there had joined a law firm as a very junior apprentice. But the old ties were still strong and into the army he went as a part time soldier, where the same intelligence and drive that had served him in civilian life raised him to the rank of sergeant.

From there his luck deserted him, and cut off from his unit he had wandered south, unwilling, unable to surrender.

Mandel's life also had humble origins but his drive and ambition had led him into politics where he had thrived.

Dodd shook his head at some of the tales Mandel had told him.

'I tried, Matthew, I tried to the very last to fight and if the fates are kind I will continue to try. France has for the moment rejected me but I have not rejected France.'

Dodd, ever practical, pointed out that he could do nothing while marching in stolen boots and that they must find a place of safety and friendly faces. And so, they continued to march south with the land rising before them until one day rising to the top of a hill, they saw snow-capped peaks on the horizon.

Stolen boots had led them to the Pyrenees.

Georges Mandel had an eye for beauty and the scene before him was undoubtedly beautiful. A river, blue with dissolved oxygen, roared down a twisting, cliff-edged valley strewn with rocks and hardy trees. A sinuous road had been cut into the side of the valley and he could see its path leading into Spain. At some time in the past a sturdy single lane bridge had been thrown across the river, and on either side of the border two small customs posts had been erected.

And that was the problem.

The bridge and the customs posts were now of little use. The Spanish customs post was little more than a hole in the ground while the French equivalent showed every sign of a hasty retreat. All that remained of the bridge were scorched stones and a single twisted pillar standing like a solitary finger mocking their hopes.

Mandel turned to his companion. 'We could still cross Matthew... perhaps if we obtained ropes?'

Dodd shook his head gloomily. 'The Asturians have been here. I'll bet it was them that blew the bridge, and if I was their commander I'd have a man or two with rifles up on those hills as lookouts. Besides the river is too fast here. We need to find another crossing point, one that's easier and one that doesn't have a road on the far side.'

Mandel looked puzzled and Dodd explained. 'The Asturians will guard the roads and have probably mined them. Even if we could cross, we would end up dead. Any guard will shoot us long before we have a chance to say we're no threat. We have to find a better, less guarded place to cross.'

'Does such a place exist Matthew?'

Dodd shrugged his shoulders, a habit he had picked up from Mandel. 'I don't know but we can't cross here so we have no choice but to move on.'

Mandel grimaced and looked at his boots, they were comfortable now but the thought of further marching made his heart sink into them. The grimace wavered and a forced smile took its place. 'Then perhaps you will lead the way Matthew.'

And so their march continued; westwards this time, away from the mountains and towards the plains that fringed the sea, the narrow river never out of earshot until an evening days later.

Their camp was nothing more than a patch of damp ground that lay under a stunted and windblown tree. An unlucky rabbit, half-cooked over a short lived fire had provided a scanty supper and Mandel slept and dreamt of better times and much better meals. His phantom repast was interrupted by a large hand clamped over his mouth. He woke instantly to see the dark shape of Dodd looming over him.

'There's someone out there!' Dodd's voice was an almost silent, hard-edged whisper but his words brought visions of a German patrol and for a moment despair became his master. For that moment it became obvious to him that he was fate's plaything, that his sense that he had a great destiny was no more than an illusion and that all their effort, the endless kilometres, the hunger and the thirst would be for nothing. So he lay by the cold fire, trying to summon up his optimism and courage while Dodd picked up his bayonet and left with only a stern injunction that Mandel should wait.

A dull rage drove Dodd as he stalked through the stunted bush, bayonet in hand. A vision of barbed wire, of endless months, even years of boredom in a camp confined with other equally bored men rose up before him. He would kill before accepting that fate.

He hunted and at last was rewarded with the silhouette of a man outlined against the glow from a thousand stars.

The solution was simple. The man would die and he would remain free. He moved forward, stealthily, silently. His hand was reaching for his enemy's forehead, his bayonet ready to slice the waiting throat when a bright light roared in front of his eyes. And then there was only darkness and a deep, deep silence.

He awoke to soft laughter and muted conversation; his head hurt and there still flashes of light pulsing in his eyes. The laughter and the conversation died as a groan rose unbidden in Dodd's throat and made an easy escape into the night air. He shook his head and put a trembling hand on the back of his head to find half-congealed blood clinging to his fingers. He blinked, trying to repel the flashes of light in his eyes.

Three sets of eyes had turned on Dodd, who saw that Mandel had been joined by two strangers; a tall, thin man with a shock of dark hair accompanied by a thickset man who held in his hand a leather cosh.

Dodd realised that this was the instrument which had caused him so much pain.

Mandel placed his hand on his friend's shoulder. 'You're awake. We thought it best to let you sleep. Matthew may I introduce Yves Massu, most recently Sargent–Chef in the Chasseurs Alpins and Stanislaw Kanski, formerly a private in the First Warsaw Grenadier Regiment. Both now have the honour to be members of the Asturian Republic's Second Guards Regiment.'

17

There was a burst of conversation from the sturdy Chasseur and Mandel translated. 'Sargent Massu is most sorry that he hurt you, and hopes that you will forgive him but there was no time to explain, and as you were about to kill his friend...'

Dodd shook his head in confusion, causing the lights in his eye to return. 'Georges what are the Asturians doing on the French side of the border?'

Mandel's teeth gleamed in the starlight. 'It would seem the Asturian commander is a most wise man; he wishes to know not only what is happening on his side of the border but on this side, so he sends out men like these two excellent individuals to spy. And who better to send? Sargent Massu speaks fluent Spanish, and Private Kanski is most learned in the German language.'

Dodd's dazed mind cleared for an instant. 'That means they have crossed the river, there is a way over!'

The teeth gleamed even brighter. 'Even so Matthew, and what is better I have explained who I am and my hopes for France. Sargent Massu has most kindly agreed to cut short their reconnaissance and escort us back over the border. Our journey, Matthew, is nearly over.'

FRIENDS

The drab paint work and antiquated guns did not deceive the Hood. The ship was but a warrior for the working day and newly fledged at that. Yet she bore the flag proudly and did her duty as best she might. Her charges were well shepherded and closed up. And for that she would give respect.

'Your convoy looks well sister.'

'Thank you, do you journey far?'

'North sister, far to the north, and you?'

'Eastwards this day, ever eastwards.'

'And you have had no trouble?'

There was pride in the steamship's answer. 'None that is beyond me.'

The Hood felt her sister's pride. This one had been born for trade but had put on her warrior's cloak, determined to yield nothing in courage.

'That I can see sister, and if trouble should strike?'

'Then I will do my duty.'

It was a stern answer and one she would have given herself. Truly this was a sister.

The distance between them was widening now but there was still time for a few last words. 'We must part now; yet I would say that if ever help is needed you have but to call.'

The steamships reply was grave and short. 'Thank you but I fear no enemy.'

The Hoods reply was equally short. 'Nor should you, goodbye.'

It was weeks later that she heard the ship's shout of defiance float over the water, heard her challenge and felt her death.

But by that time she was too far away to help the Rawalpindi.

'Ah my friend is this not foolish of us?'

The Hood heard the voice of the Dunkerque who was far on the horizon. The French Battlecruiser's voice was a joyous thing, though muffled by the fogs and rains which infested Norwegian waters.

'With but a little effort we could both be in warmer seas. I sailed them last year and very pleasant it was. I would have those days again. Instead I am here with the seals and the whales and only a weak sun to warm my deck. Now in the south there is a sun that is not a pale ghost but a mighty orb that shines down. Wherever I went I was admired and praised.'

The Hood laughed. 'And you loved every moment I imagine.'

A very light, almost girlish giggle floated across the water. 'But of course my friend, I did indeed love every moment of it, and let us be honest I received no more than my due. For am I not beautiful? My lines are graceful, my paintwork is beyond reproach, I combine speed, and power with an ability to enforce my will on others. Am I to be blamed for this? Of course not.'

The Hood felt just a little lighter for hearing her friend's self-mocking words but she knew that under the frivolous manner lay a warrior with a sense of honour and duty as deeply rooted as was her own.

Despite that she tried to follow her friends gentle teasing. 'And if some of that marvellous paintwork was damaged, say by an enemy?'

The Dunkerque mimicked hurt and outrage. 'My friend now it is you who joke, surely you know that it would be my pleasure to make sure that full payment would be made for any attempt to alter my complexion. Such an insult would be punished most severely. My crew who love me as they love their mothers would insist upon it.'

The Hood laughed. 'All that for paint '!

The Dunkerque laughed with her. 'My friend you make fun of me. My paint is very precious to me that is true but I, like you hold my honour more precious still. And my duty demands that I stay here shivering, waiting for an enemy who may never come. And that my friend is why I long for the sun.'

An Arctic blast heeled the Hood over and as the icy water reluctantly poured from her she began to think that possibly her friend had made a very good point indeed.

Her sisters were dead. They had died like cattle brought to the slaughter or bravely, with their faces to the foe.

And she was dying, she could feel the sea surging through her, feel the last thoughts of her crew. But she was not yet dead. Her battle ensigns still flew, her hearts still beat and her guns still fired.

Again, and again she stabbed at her adversary, again and again she was punished for her audacity. She was not without reward; some of her lunges struck home and though she might be dying there was much blood on the sea and not all of it was hers. No miracle could save her and she knew it. There was only one path she could follow now and she walked along it gladly. A last flurry of gunfire and she was finished, she had done all that flesh and steel could do.

The sea claimed her and took her to rest.

Her labours were over and H.M.S Acasta joined her sisters.

They had waited, the Hood and the Dunkerque. Storms has lashed at them, time had gnawed on them. Convoys had come and gone, shielded by their power. A whole campaign had blossomed in hope and died in despair. Sisters they had left behind, their voices forever stilled. But they still lived, though untried and untested.

And today their bows pointed to the south and home.

'The sun, my friend the sun! Already I feel warmer, every beat of my hearts brings me closer to home and blessed warmth! May the sun burn from me the memories of this unprofitable place.'

The Dunkerque was a little ahead of her and nearly fifteen miles nearer the coast of Norway. Trondheim, now lost and occupied lay ahead of them and would be the point where their paths would diverge.

The Hood felt both the excitement and the discontent of her friend. In truth she too would feel happier when tied up in friendly home port. It had indeed been an unprofitable time. Out here in these sunless waters they had chased twin phantoms, ghosts who appeared, killed and vanished again. Their dead sisters remained unavenged and unsatisfied. She could only hope for better times.

The two ships and their escorts chattered back and forth and each turn of their propellers took them further south and further away from an accursed campaign.

And to the point where their courses diverged.

They said their farewells and the Hood and the Foxhound turned westwards and to home. But only for a few moments.

'My friend?' The Dunkerque's voice had an edge to it and the jovial tone was now entirely missing. 'My friend if it would not inconvenience you I would be glad of your company once more.'

The Hood was instantly alert to her friend's voice. 'There is trouble?'

'Perhaps my friend, perhaps. My escort reported smoke and went to investigate and found an enemy. Naturally we are attacking. Audace, toujours de l'audace, n'est-ce pas? But there is a problem.'

'Oh?'

'It is no little enemy I am about to attack. One enemy I do not fear but my escort has reported that my opponent does not travel alone. It seems that she has a sister.'

A thrill of anticipation ran through the Hood. 'Our ghosts have arrived.'

'So it would seem. I suspect they wish to make for port. Alas for them, I lie between them and safety. My friend one enemy I do not fear but two? So if it would not inconvenience you I would welcome your assistance.'

The Dunkerque's last words were wasted because the Hood and the Foxhound were already cutting foaming circles in the sea and pointing speeding bows towards their friends.

It could not be considered an office, it was far too small for such a title. Indeed Pulver imagined there were dog kennels that were not only larger but better appointed. But this cramped space was all he had to complete the forms without which the Hood would apparently cease to function. Rosters, spares requisitions, fuel consumption reports, fitness and conduct files; all had to be meticulously completed and fed to a system which ate them without seeming effort.

He ran a very small part of the engineering space, a tiny part of a much greater whole and already he was being suffocated by paperwork. So he sat on a chair specifically designed to cause him pain and laboriously wrote reports while his mind had visions of home and grey-green eyes. He could now truthfully look into those eyes and say that he had never been in any danger. Indeed so calm had this cruise been that he had been in more danger of boredom than anything else.

His musings were interrupted by two sounds.

The first was the raucous sound of the bell that called him to action stations, the second more subtle but equally exciting. It was the soft whoomph of more boilers being fired up, followed seconds later by the high whine of the turbines spooling up.

He felt the ship heeling over as she began her turn.

Within seconds he was at his station, hands poised over controls, ready for orders, the long practised actions now ingrained in him. He glanced over at Leading Seaman Stebbings who merely nodded that he and the rest of his crew were ready.

He had forgotten about paperwork now, even the grey-green eyes were a dim memory. All that mattered now was that this was where he was meant to be. He was with his ship and she was with him.

They were closed up for action stations and Jack McIntyre was enveloped in the white anti-flash gear that duty and common sense compelled him to wear. The tight fitting hood still gave him a good view of the Hood nearby as she picked up speed. Smoke poured from her funnels and the wave that clung to her bow rose higher and higher. She was striding through the water with longer and longer steps but still the Foxhound was leaving her behind.

The Foxhound would get there first.

And strangely that did not frighten him.

Jack watched fascinated as water sprang up like great trees that had risen from some secret place on the sea floor and sought the sunlight. This was the second salvo aimed at the Foxhound and was just as disturbingly accurate as the first had been. Water and debris rained down on her as she closed the distance between her and the giant that was trying to kill her.

Two miles away the French destroyer was closing in even faster, and although her firing had slackened from its original frenzy she still had her teeth firmly into her opponent.

Her mission was the same as the Foxhound's. Distract the enemy, make it impossible for her to concentrate on the Dunkerque who was already exchanging fire with her own enemy.

The two ships forced their foe to constantly move, whenever she tried to steady on a set course, French or British shells struck her or torpedoes lunged at her. Jack did not know if the Foxhound was engaged with the Scharnhorst or the Gneisenau but ultimately it did not matter for their opponent was to be given no peace, no respite, the two destroyers clinging to her sides like vicious wolves.

A salvo of Torpedoes left the Foxhound, combing through the water, eager to complete their journey, eager to kill, and once again her opponent swung sharply, still trying to destroy these impudent attackers.

The dance continued with both destroyers slashing at the German ship with their guns. It was a deadly dance, where one misstep, one late turn meant death.

The larger French ship staggered and her boat deck disappeared in a fog of sparks and Jack was sure she would sink but she straightened on her course, still pouring fire into her assailant.

At last both ships broke away from their enemy, racing away, and Jack looked anxiously around, certain that his ship had been hit and in his excitement he had missed a mortal wound. He could see nothing but the increasing distance between them and their still angry opponent and his fears were replaced with puzzlement.

His ship was peppered with shrapnel and their French companion showed no signs of further damage; they weren't even retreating under the cover of a smoke screen.

Jack was about to comment on the strangeness of the situation when overhead there was an eerie rumbling sound. Moments later eight fifteen inch shells plunged into the water around the German ship.

The Hood had arrived.

She ran past her friend who was locked in combat.

'I am a little hurt' was the reply to the Hood's question. 'And my paintwork, my beautiful, beautiful paint work is quite ruined.' The Dunkerque's voice then took on a sombre tone, and there was sadness in her voice that she had never heard before. 'And my crew, men I have sworn to protect and keep from harm, are hurt and dying. And for that there will be payment my friend, I will extract much payment for this day. But our escorts, though brave are suffering. Perhaps it would be as well if you relieved them of their burden.'

The Hood sped on.

She spoke to them gently, calmly.

She thanked the great engines that had brought her to this place. She praised the turbines that spun so happily. She gave words of encouragement to the great guns who must speak this day. Her words touched them all.

All of them were her. All of them made her what she was.

Only her children were unhappy. 'It's not fair,' they said. 'We should go closer and then we could play.'

The Hood understood their frustration but today she would stand off, out of range of her enemy's guns and pound her. It was a poor warrior who gave her enemy an advantage. Today her four point five guns must remain silent but how to placate her exuberant children?

She put on her most soothing voice. 'I know it is not fair but if I go closer, I may get hurt, others may die. That I cannot allow, for they are under my protection. I know that you would serve well and faithfully and there will come a day when only you stand between me and my enemies but that day is not today. If I go closer I break my oath to guard all from keel to mast. Would you have me break my oath?'

There was a long drawn out silence and then a reluctant but understanding chorus of acknowledgement.

She thanked them and began a sweeping curve that would place her guns pointing directly at her enemy. She heard the firing computers talking, felt the fifteen inch barrels reaching out to touch the sky and then she shook as the shells left her body.

She was the Hood.

And today an enemy would die.

'Under.' The Petty Officer's voice was that of a spectator.

They had done their part for now and were watching the Hood seek out the German ship.

'Last one was over, so the next lot'll win the coconut.'

The next salvo from the Hood was a little behind the target and Jack watched as giant fists plunged down into the sea in a line of tall spray. Only the last fist hit the target and the aft turret of their enemy was smashed open.

'Told you. Now he has a choice,' was the only comment from the laconic seaman.

Jack watched as the ship turned and presented her stern to them, hastened on her way by another salvo of fifteen inch shells.

'Very sensible.' There was an approving nod from Jack's companion. 'Just what I'd have done myself.'

'But why is he running away, why doesn't he fight?'

There was a half mocking smile before the answer. 'Fight? Fight when you're out gunned and outnumbered, and your mate is already half sunk? Don't be daft lad. The Hood's already shown she can hit, and if I was her I wouldn't let anyone close the range too fast. By the time she gets the Hood in range, she'll just be floating scrap iron. No Jack she'll run and run fast, and live to fight another day. That way we have to devote ships to counter her and she'll always be a worry. Mind you,' he said reflectively.' I wouldn't like to be in her captain's shoes when old Adolph hears about this.'

He gave a short laugh. 'Running away from a fight? Langsdorf shot himself rather than face Hitler and that may be his best option. Now my bet is that we go and help the Dunkerque and make sure that we get a kill.'

And that is what they got.

The Dunkerque's opponent could not withstand the fire from both allied Battlecruisers, and though she fought with courage she was burnt and blasted into wreckage. In less than an hour, with flags still flying, she turned on her side and laid herself to rest with all her recent victims.

Jack forced himself to look as the sea put out the raging fires and filled the gaping holes. It was a sight that filled him with horror. Only the atonement of picking up the pitifully few survivors diluted that horror.

And not by much.

She had fired her guns in anger and some at least of her dead sisters had been avenged. She had vindicated herself and confirmed a friendship.

'I am not too badly hurt,' her friend had told her. 'A week or two in the dockyards and I will be more beautiful than ever.'

They had laughed together, these friends, these warriors bound together in battle.

And then for the second time they parted. The voice of the Dunkerque came from far over the waves. 'Au revoir mon ami, may we meet again.'

A week.

That was all the Hood was given.

A week to resupply, to repair and to mend. A week to gaze at the land on which they were forbidden to tread and to write letters to loved ones who for the moment existed only as memories.

And then South, where her power was needed and new enemies had arisen. South to where an ally was faltering. South to the Mediterranean. Where they would meet again but only in the deep sadness of France quitting the war.

'Please!' Her voice was filled with tears. 'Please do as they ask, come fight with me as once we did. We still have enemies.'

From seven miles away came the reply. 'I wish it could be so my friend but what you ask cannot be.'

'Please!'

'My friend I cannot.'

'Then come with me far across the sea and wait for better days.'

Again the reply sang over the sea. 'With you my friend escorting me as if I was defeated, with my hearts barely beating, with a pitiful wave under my bow?'

'No! It would not be like that, I would never...'

'I know you would not my friend but I have my pride and above that, always above that, I have my honour.'

'You would keep your honour, it would not be lost. Please I beg you.'

'My friend I would ask you one question.'

'Yes?'

'If the situation were reversed, if you were here and I was outside with guns trained would you submit?'

There could only be one answer, though it was torn from her. 'No.' The reply had a wry and wistful smile.

'Exactly, what must be, will be, my friend. You would wish otherwise I know.' There was a great sigh from her friend which pierced the Hood's armoured sides and lodged in her soul. 'I must go now; my crew needs me even as yours needs you. Au revoir mon ami.'

'No, wait!'

There was no reply, and she knew she would never speak to the Dunkerque again.

Dully she began the hateful preparations. There was no enthusiasm in what she did only a growing sense of horror.

But her shells killed.

Killed her friend.

The silence had been deafening.

Her guns no longer sped death over the miles but hung mute in terrible sadness. Her crew moved like ghosts within her or gazed at the pall of smoke that rose from the distant shore. She had done this. She had killed. She had murdered. Not in hot blood, not some dark and angry enemy but a friend one who traded jest with jest, laughter with laughter. The jests were twisted steel now, and laughter was lost in the oily smoke.

Only curses and recriminations came from the shore now and every one of them struck her with terrible force. She was duty and service and those words were as much a part of her as her greatest frame or smallest rivet and by those laws it was her duty to kill her friend. But those laws were of little comfort to her now as she turned away from the hateful shore.

She roamed the inland sea, from east to west, from north to south, her friend's last words echoing within her. Each day she taunted the enemy, and each day the taunts grew more insulting. But only silence greeted her words and her enemies remained sheltered, secure and immovable. Ports were visited, convoys received her strength but that which was most needed eluded her. Only blood could wash away the burden that lay on her soul, only an enemy's destruction could avenge her friend's death, and she was denied it.

She was duty and service, and for now she must cling to that but she promised herself that the Dunkerque would be avenged.

And only on that day would she be able to say goodbye to her friend.

MEETINGS

Jorge had seen them walk into the room and his hand went to the heavy revolver that was strapped to his waist. He hated them, these suited killers. They were responsible for the burnt villages, the spoilt crops and the many, many deaths. He would put a bullet in every one of them. Better yet they would die with his hands around their throats, eyes bulging, lungs gasping as they paid just once for their many sins.

And he could not.

He could not, though every atom of his soul screamed for revenge. His hand fell from his pistol and his breathing slowed.

There must be no more burnt villages, crops must once more burst towards the light and above all there must be no more deaths. And if his strangled need for vengeance was the price he had to pay then he would pay it. Through clenched teeth undoubtedly but he would pay it.

And to add humour to the situation, the Fascists thought that the advantage still lay with him. He'd used the last of the French aid to smash the final Fascist army and after that his drive east met no resistance. The war still spluttered on, patrol still met patrol in bloody skirmishes, the occasional bomber from both sides still hailed death on an exhausted enemy but the armies clashed no more. But the Fascists did not know just how exhausted his people were. Nor could they tell with certainty just how much aid had flowed south before it was cut off forever.

He had built wooden tanks that were carelessly left where prying eyes could see them from a distance. Radios told of phantom units and of supplies that did not exist. Aircraft flying on carefully hoarded petrol moved from airfield to airfield, mimicking a force many times greater. He was still a master of subterfuge, a man whose greatest asset was his enemy's fear.

And so an offer had come from Madrid.

Not peace, still less a recognition that the Asturians and the Basques were free but an armistice, a small and uncertain cessation in the killing.

And now these sleek emissaries of the arch killer had watched him unstrap the pistol and place it out of reach. They watched him swallow the bitter hate, and erase the memory of dead comrades. They watched him with just a hint of nervousness tinting their smiles.

The politicians, the people who governed Asturias from bomb shattered buildings, were a known quantity. They were men who thought along familiar lines but the man in the stained sheepskin coat with the battered binoculars slung round his neck was an unknown factor.

He smiled at them, showing his teeth, watching with amusement their almost imperceptible flinching. It was why he was here, he did not need his pistol to frighten these men; his smile was more than enough. It was the smile of a man who had outfought and out generaled every opponent sent against him. While he was in the room Franco's delegates would be on edge and he hoped would be just little bit clumsy, a little less abrasive. His smile would be his country's armour and her sword.

He looked across the table at the chief Spanish delegate and gave him his very best smile.

The morning sunshine was weak and uncertain but very welcome.

For days now he had sat in a poorly lit room while offer and counter offer bounced from every wall. That there would be agreement he did not doubt but no one in the room believed that peace could be achieved. Too many compromises would have to be made, too many dearly held ideas would have to change. The best, the very best that could be achieved would be a pause while each side rebuilt and looked for allies, new or old.

The thought depressed him, for though he had found a talent for war, there had grown within him a distaste for it. So he walked through the streets of Gijón, pleased to see that the rubble was being cleared and that eyes no longer looked up to the skies in fear. He had no destination, no set route. Instead he let his feet choose where he went while his mind wandered far from the city.

Allies.

That one thought dominated his every waking moment and coloured his dreams.

France was no more and might drift from reluctant ally to outright enemy. He had blown every bridge and mined every road between them but a border he had once longed to reach was now a danger. Russia was now locked into an alliance with Germany and was waiting on the edge of a war which grew more bloody every day. No help could come from there.

Which left only a group of islands poised on the edge of a cold Atlantic. Those islands still fought, undaunted and unbowed and still spat defiance at the Fascists but with all their energies directed at mere survival what aid could they give?

It was a maze without an exit. No matter how far he walked the answer eluded him.

The argument broke into his thoughts. His blind wandering had brought him to the building that was used as the home of the Asturian government. In happier times it had been a school and echoed to the sounds of children. Now it was a sandbagged fortress and echoed to the sounds of angry voices. It seemed the sentries were refusing to allow entrance to four men insisting that they be given admittance.

He was about to walk by, the argument being no concern of his but he noticed that two of the men wore the shoulder flashes of the Second Guards Regiment. These were men from France and Poland who had poured across the border with the sounds of blown bridges behind them. They were, to a man, fanatical haters of Fascists and normally extremely disciplined, so seeing such a public display intrigued him.

He walked over, and the sentries seeing the famous sheepskin coat stiffened and the loud voices ceased.

He kept his voice mild. There was little point in inflaming already raw tempers. 'Just what is going on here?'

They would never have found the crossing point.

It was so well hidden that they would have passed it without a second glance. A few well-placed stones and a sunken rope that was easily pulled taut was their passport over the border. From there it was but a short journey to Gijón.

They had passed through the signs of war, makeshift crosses over piles of freshly dug earth, burnt houses by the hundred but it was not until they came to Gijón that they saw true devastation because Franco's forces had tried to bomb the city into submission.

And failed.

The city was returning to life. There seemed to be an almost instinctive urge to repair it. Mandel saw a thin girl, battered doll in one hand and equally battered bucket in the other walk up to a small cart and after carefully placing the doll where it could come to no harm empty the bucket of rubble into the cart. After picking up her doll she returned to the crowd of people who were pulling apart the remains of a bombed out building.

Mandel was impressed. Even the children were part of a city returning to life.

But though much had changed in Gijón some things remained the same. The guards at the government buildings had their orders and nothing would change the fact that without orders or the proper paperwork there would be no admittance to see any government official. Mandel could with difficulty follow the high speed exchange of arguments and insults which took place between Massu and the sentries, while Dodd was completely lost in the jungle of Castilian Spanish.

It was an impasse; the papers given at the border had no validity here in Asturias and without them Mandel and Dodd were just another two lost refugees.

The argument swayed back and forth, rising in tempo and anger until it died not slowly but in the middle of the Asturian sentry describing in some detail just what Sargent Massu's mother did for a living and why she was so successful at it.

Mandel turned and saw a young man in a grease-stained, sheepskin coat looking at him with amused eyes.

The man interrogated the obviously worried sentries who answered with great formality. He nodded, seeming satisfied with their answers and Mandel's hopes which had begun to rise fell again. This man, despite his disreputable appearance was obviously a person of some rank and equally obviously had accepted the sentries' explanation.

The man turned once more to the two travellers and Mandel was surprised to see he spoke not to him but to Dodd. Mandel translated and Dodd reluctantly handed over the rifle which had never left his side. The rifle was given a thorough inspection and given back to its obviously relieved owner.

"You look after your rifle very well,' translated Mandel.

Dodd, confused, wondered just what answer to give to this strange man. Finally he could come up with nothing more than the fact that he was a British soldier, an answer which seemed to please the man who then turned to ask who they were and why they had travelled so far.

It was not a long explanation but Mandel gave emphasis to what he believed was his great mission.

'I have never heard of you,' began the man "…but then I am a simple peasant and have been a little busy of late. Do you think you can do all that you wish?'

'I can only try,' replied Mandel cautiously, a little annoyed that his fame had failed to reach this part of the world.

The man nodded his approval. 'It is all any of us can do.'

He closed his eyes for a moment, obviously thinking very hard.

The sentries quivered a little as he turned to them. 'Do you see these men?'

'Why yes General of course we see them, that is why we refused them entry, we…'

The man shook his head very emphatically. 'Do you see these men?'

'Yes general…that is…no, General.'

A great smile was their reward. 'A good answer; for how could you; they were never here. For that matter nor was I and if asked that is exactly what you will say…is that not so?'

'Yes General.'

He turned and gave orders to Sargent Massu and his companion, swearing them also to silence and they departed with the man's words of praise locked forever within them.

Dodd remained puzzled, cursing the fact that his lack of knowledge of any foreign language beyond a little bad French had locked him out of the conversation. He whispered a question to Mandel who, though he had already guessed the answer, translated it for the general.

There was a grin from the man. 'I am known by many names - some of them not very complimentary - but my mother called me Jorge. And you are my guests and I am at your service.'

The grin transformed itself into an enigmatic smile. 'And I hope that soon you will be able to return the favour.'

Jorge lit a precious candle which did its best to hold back the growing night. 'Electricity is limited in Gijón,' he explained 'and even the temporary home of a general must take its turn.'

They had bathed and eaten, and though the meal was simple it was very welcome. Dodd was dozing peacefully, his head resting on his chest which rose and fell at regular intervals. Jorge had sat back in his chair, vanishing into the shadows so that his voice appeared to be disembodied.

'I apologise for kidnapping you so abruptly but you must realise that your arrival here is potentially very dangerous both for you and my country. We have fought a war, a successful war but one that has been very damaging.' A grim note entered the voice now. 'I do not think that Asturias can afford any more victories. We must stop fighting and allow ourselves a little time to breathe. And while we breathe we must kill the demons that war has allowed to slumber.'

'Demons?' Mandel was a little confused. Perhaps the wine that Jorge had given them was stronger than he thought.

'Demons'; insisted Jorge. 'Did I not use the right word? Is it not so in your country when what a man thinks condemns him in the eyes of another? I am a simple man but even I can see that the strains of peace are more terrible than the strains of war. So now we must build a nation out many different beliefs. This will be hard, though perhaps with enemies on all sides, we will be given little time to do so. But still we must try.'

A harsh chuckle escaped from the darkness of the chair.

'But not with you here Señor Mandel. You are a distraction. There are those who would claim you as their own; others who would seek to put you on trial - all would seek to use you for their own purposes.

My President's work is difficult enough without a person such as yourself being here, so you must go and go soon, before you are discovered. To journey on is what you most desire. So we are in agreement?'

'My country needs me.'

'As mine needs me,' agreed Jorge. 'Yet your country used mine for its own needs and others too have used us as a scourge. This must stop, and I and my president have certain thoughts that we wish you to convey. Will you do this for us. Will you be our messenger? Better than that, will you be our friend?'

Mandel thought for a moment. To be a messenger was no great hardship. Besides he was in this man's power; agreement seemed sensible.

'Of course, General, I would be honoured to be your emissary.'

'Then I will tell you what we wish. This is what we will need when this peace is broken as broken it must be.'

Jorge began to speak and Mandel realised that as he suspected the man, despite his assertions of being a simple peasant, was far from stupid. Un educated certainly but Jorge had a firm grasp of his own world and his place in it.

And as Mandel listened and the night grew darker, he heard Jorge's plans for the new nation that had sprung up on the shores of the Bay of Biscay. He heard of the struggles and the deaths, and the blood that would not surrender. Jorge's last words tumbled out with a plea that his nation should live and Mandel realised that although his heart belonged to France he had found a small corner of it that would beat for Asturias.

He would deliver the message. For Asturias of course but also for France.

Always for France.

The tall man stood in his office, his voice booming and implacable. There was no sense in him that he was in any way beholden to the red-faced man who sat behind the desk. Instead he acted as if the whole might of France and her empire lay under his command, obedient to his every wish.

He did not treat the man as an equal, or even as a man who had his own cares but as a subordinate...and not a very intelligent one at that. Impossible demands and statements which defied reality flowed from him in a never-ending stream. How much of this was a bold front and how much was due to his personality was impossible to say but what was certain was that the sympathy which had greeted the man on his arrival was wearing away fast.

The man believed that he had a destiny, that he was a man whose time had come. He traded on his rarity, used it as a coin of his own realm, certain that its value could never be debased or denied.

Adjustments had been made for his beliefs, excuses had been accepted for his outbursts but his paranoia and distrust of allies both actual and potential were becoming liabilities. The man behind the desk looked up at the cold face and willed his blood pressure down, by another effort killing the angry words which clawed for release.

With grim politeness he tried to impress on the man that insulting the Americans was a game which no one could win, and that perhaps a period of calm, if not of diplomacy, would produce better results.

The reaction was all he had come to expect and the discussion ended with a door being slammed shut behind an angry departing Frenchman.

Churchill sighed and as he sighed the last of his anger died and a regretful sorrow took its place.

De Gaulle was a necessary counterpoint to the Vichy government, and whatever his views on the recognition of Vichy by the Americans he was still the only option. At least he thought so. Washington had vastly different ideas about the man and that was causing problems.

Another sigh escaped Churchill's lips. This latest outburst would have to be smoothed over with the Americans, which would further weaken his position.

He was caught. He needed both De Gaulle and Washington.

And there were other problems to be dealt with, all of them urgent, many of them almost unsolvable. For a moment though he indulged himself and ignored them and pulled out a purple folder with an innocuous title. He chuckled. No one would guess that these reports from the Joint Technical Board concealed not dry paperwork but tales of espionage and daring which would do credit to the most hackneyed of novels.

The reports appealed to the romantic pirate in him which he could now only experience at second hand. He read briskly. Plans were being made and preparations were proceeding with gratifying speed. He would indeed set Europe ablaze.

And then almost at the last page were a few lines, a request for passage for two men who had escaped from France. The paragraph was nothing out of the ordinary, merely a transfer of the funds required to place the men on an aircraft. He was about to gloss over it. This was obviously not the stimulus he needed but then he noted a name that he knew.

His mind took him back to a meeting in France. He remembered pale faces and panicked voices but there was one undaunted voice that did not panic and though the voice was never raised it preached continued resistance and regarded surrender with scorn. That voice had vanished, lost in the maelstrom of defeat but now it had appeared again and once more he heard the words.

The germ of an idea grew, slowly at first but then, as the showman who was never far from the surface began to appear, it blossomed with great suddenness.

This should be big, a triumph, something dramatic something that would bestow dominance and authority both on the giver and the recipient. It should be an entrance that would be remembered; the man must certainly not be delivered in some mundane manner.

He drew deeply on his cigar, hoping that its smoke would inspire him. He followed an errant wisp of smoke as it travelled across the room and finally exhausted itself against a map of Southern Europe. He knew then just what kind of entrance he would give the undaunted voice. And this would bring a little sorely needed balance to a situation which was fast becoming intolerable.

His fingers reached out and pressed a yellowed, much used switch. 'First Sea Lord please.'

There was a click and he spoke rapidly explaining his need.

'So, what do you have that could be used?'

'You do?'

'A refit?'

'Yes, she would do well enough, in fact she could hardly be bettered.'

'Yes, please be kind enough to give the orders.'

'Thank you.'

The phone was placed back in its cradle and he knew that he had done his best to give the man a worthy re-entry into the vortex of French politics.

It would be a dramatic and well publicised entrance, he would see to that. It would not be enough he knew but it would be a start, a very good start indeed.

He puffed reflectively on the last of the cigar and addressed his last comment to the now departed De Gaulle. 'Indispensable, are you? Well perhaps not!'

There was a new man sitting at the table when Dodd and Mandel woke that morning. He was deep in conversation with Jorge but rose as they entered the room and examined the two newcomers. A deep blue shirt covered the man's chest but Dodd concentrated on the man's eyes. They were an intense, ice blue. There was no warmth in them and he realised that he was being appraised in the same way a butcher looks at an animal in the moments before his knife begins to work.

He shivered and wondered if Jorge had changed his mind and their journey would end today in a forgotten grave. But Jorge smiled and spoke what was obviously a morning greeting and once more Dodd cursed his lack of any language skills.

He smiled back at the man and allowed the talk to flow past him. There was a final burst of conversation, and Mandel began to translate what had been said.

'This is Comandante O'Neil, Matthew he is…' He looked at Jorge once more and asked a question. Jorge touched his face and grinned, his voice full of humour. 'Jorge says that the Comandante is his ears and his eyes…perhaps Chief of Security?

'In any event Matthew the Comandante has arranged for us to be smuggled into Portugal where he has many contacts and from there he hopes we can be flown back to England. You are going home Matthew.'

Dodd blinked for a moment as Mandel's words registered. He tried in comical Spanish to thank Jorge who laughed and grasped him by the shoulders. 'It is nothing,' translated Mandel. 'Any man who can keep a rifle as clean as yours deserves my help and you are welcome to return at any time...so long as you bring your rifle with you.'

And so began their journey west, along dirt roads and in third class railway carriages, their guides ever-changing, some sullen and silent, others smiling and talkative. The miles and the days passed under their feet until one day they sat at an anonymous cafe in a tiny fishing village, waiting to turn south and begin their voyage to Lisbon.

A man slid into the seat next to them and began to read the paper and although he kept his eyes firmly on the news he began to speak. 'There has been a change in plans, Senors. Your journey ends here. In two days' time you will board the fishing boat Santa Maria when she takes her usual run and from there you will be picked up.'

Mandel brought his coffee cup to his lips and tried to appear unconcerned. 'Picked up? Where? Who is picking us up?'

'I do not know Senor. It is better that I do not know, and for now it is better that you do not know.'

Silently Mandel fumed. He was growing tired of this game of hide and seek for which he believed he was totally unsuited but there was little point in antagonising the man so he sighed and made sure that at least he and Dodd had a bed for the night.

And for two days they waited. in ignorance, the cramped walls of the tiny airless room pressing in on them, the sounds of everyday life mocking them until at last they were released and taken to the jetty.

The fishing boat was less than clean and the crew matched the state of the boat. There was no attempt at conversation. Dodd and Mandel were roughly thrust into the hold with only each other and the smell of rotting fish for company while the engine began to move them away from the jetty and into the black night.

They never knew what course the boat had taken. They could only wait, listening to the occasional order in harsh Portuguese and the constant throb of the engine. For hours they waited, the air in the hold growing thicker and staler until at last the boat seemed to slow.

There were voices now and Dodd fancied that he heard English being spoken as well.

The hatch cover was pulled back and they were unceremoniously pulled from their captivity and thrust into the arms of a young man who seemed equally anxious to transfer them to a boat pulled up alongside them. Dodd had a brief vision of armed sailors before their new home picked up speed and left the fishing boat far behind. It was only moments later that he could sense something solid looming up out of the darkness. Their boat slowed, pulled up alongside the shape and was dragged up its sides. He could see little and could only get an impression of massive steel plates sliding by as they rose through the air to arrive with a thump and jangle of chains.

He heard Mandel asking questions but they went unanswered and both were thrust into a tiny cabin to sleep as best they could.

It was full daylight when they were awakened and taken along a maze of corridors and steep stairs to what was obviously the bridge of a large warship. Alongside two smaller ships kept station and in front of them they could see massive guns pointing forward towards any potential enemy.

A steward thrust mugs of steaming cocoa into their hands and a tall man slid off his seat and thrust out his hand.

'Welcome to the Hood gentleman.'

Dodd could only grin back.

He was going home.

CHANGES IN COURSES

He had picked up the music box in Alexandria where it had sat forlorn and almost forgotten on a shelf in a back-street shop a long way from the bars which housed most of the Hood's crew. He had removed layers of long neglected dust, grimacing a little as the dirt stuck to his fingers.

The box was covered in leather, thick and old, and very, very black. Cut into the leather was a figure of a man on a camel who was staring dolefully at a group of wilting palm trees. It was not an attractive picture and he had been about to place it back on the shelf when some impulse made him open the box.

And another world was revealed to him.

The inside was lined with shining red silk and thin slivers of mother of pearl and tortoiseshell that swirled in pleasing patterns. Pulver was convinced that though the outside of the box had been made by very rough hands indeed the inside was the work of a master craftsman.

His hands fumbled with the key and the box seemed to sneeze, ejecting decades of silence and then with the minimum of fuss the tiny drum began to turn and shards of sound flew through the air. The familiar tune decided him; the box would be his messenger when the owner of those grey-green eyes played the song she would know his intent.

The haggling over the box was half-hearted and he was sure that if he had pushed he could have got the box for a much reduced price but the box was his from the moment it threw out those first notes.

And now the carefully wrapped box was secure beside him in the berth that gave scant regard to privacy and even less to space. He drew the coarse grey curtain and tried to sleep but sleep laughed and hid, leaving him alone with his thoughts.

After the sinking of The Gneisenau, they had been considered heroes. There had been headlines and honours; medals had been flung about like rice at society wedding.

But now they were going home with quite a different battle behind them. Mers-el-Kébir had been a massacre, the French fleet slaughtered at anchor.

What would the grey-green eyes think of him now, would she still see the hero or would she see the blood dripping from his fingers? Would she welcome him or would she scorn the box and its musical message?

War was not supposed to be like this. War was black or it was white, good or bad. But deep in the bowels of the ship, his ship, he had felt the guns kill and later he had seen the columns of smoke that marked the places where friends had died. Was he warrior or murderer? The question rumbled in his mind, never finding a place to rest.

His ship turned the waves into a gentle motion that forced sleep to give him what he needed. He slept and dreamt of death and music boxes, of grey-green eyes and a ship that sang with words that few could understand. And as he slept his ship slipped her moorings and turned her head north.

Pulver was going home.

Geordie settled back in the seat and prepared to be bored. This was Mabel's idea of what a good film should be but certainly not his. A good western or maybe a gangster film with Jimmy Cagney or Paul Muni would have him on the edge of his seat but Mabel had chosen a romance and what excitement could there be in such a film? Why there wouldn't be a single shoot-out in the whole two hours that he was condemned to sit there!

Still the evening wasn't a total loss. Pathé News had shown the Hood in port dropping off some French bloke that he'd never heard of. The announcer had made a big deal of the man's arrival, praising his heroic escape from France and hinting that this meant a change in direction in Free French politics.

Frankly Geordie wasn't interested what the French, free or otherwise, got up to but he was interested in the Hood and eagerly lapped up the few seconds of film that showed her. She looked good and he had felt a surge of pride as he remembered the work that had gone into her.

The armed merchant cruisers and occasional destroyers that the yards saw these days filled men's bellies and kept their hands busy but there would never be another Hood, never again would they have the time to put so much effort into a single project.

The film ground on, and Geordie fidgeted in his seat earning him a dirty look from Mabel. He grinned in the darkness and waited for her to become engrossed once more in the on screen drama.

He turned and looked around the cinema. It was full, which was a testament to the money which flowed through Jarrow these days, though there were more uniforms than ever in the seats. His eyes rested on a couple in the back row; like him they were not interested in the film, unlike him they had something far more interesting to do.

They made a nice couple from what he could see, a rather young naval officer and a pretty dark haired girl.

It brought back memories of his younger days and for a moment he gazed back at Mabel but she was too immersed in the Hollywood romance to consider any real life imitation. He shrugged. There was nothing much else he could do, and he consoled himself with the thought that soon his son Jack would be here.

And on the screen the love affair grew and grew.

He was not a murderer.

At least not in her eyes and he thanked God for it.

The grey-green eyes had met his and he knew that in those eyes there were no doubts. He had thrust the box into her hands urging her to play the tune that fate had decided he should pick. She looked puzzled but as the notes of Mendelson's wedding march began to fill the air the realisation of what he was asking hit her. Her eyes lit up and she threw herself into his arms. And those arms were not those of a murderer and that was what counted.

He had two weeks of leave and in those two weeks much must be done.

The grey-green eyes began to panic and frantic letters were sent out but that was not his concern. He had lit the fuse and was content now to await the explosion that would alter his life.

He had thought that an evening in the cinema watching Hitchcock's latest epic would lessen the strain on the grey-green eyes but that was not to be. He saw very little of the screen that evening but the night was hugely enjoyable none the less.

The appointment was for nine am, so Dodd with his horror of being late was lined up with a crowd of equally anxious women, each and every one of them hoping to acquire a pre-war dress or now rare shoes. The doors were flung open and he was swept along in the great tide of humanity whose members were determined to take no prisoners in the pursuit of a bargain.

He struggled to get free, his toes bruised and his ribs having had the attention of more than one elbow but at last he was able to make his way to the service lift and rise above the mayhem.

The lift rose creakily but delivered him safely to a dimly lit corridor and at the end of that corridor, as promised was a door marked 'Sales and Requisitions.'

The room was not what he expected.

Bright chintz curtains shielded the room from the winter sun and prints of hunting scenes hung on the wall. In the corner a shining kettle spluttered and steamed under blue flames. And there was a desk, a polished orderly desk and behind it sat a middle-aged man with bright red hair and a matching moustache.

The man rose and held out his hand.

Dodd is it? Glad to see you, will you take tea? Do please sit down.'

There was the noise of poured water and rattling spoons and Dodd noticed that the man had rather smoothly failed to introduce himself.

A delicate cup was placed before him and he took a sip and was surprised to find its taste very different to the tea served in the Sergeants' mess.

His face must have shown his surprise because there was a delighted chuckle from the far side of the desk.

'Lapsang Souchong, Sergeant, a tea from China. Not your ordinary tea I admit and something of an acquired taste. My grandfather of blessed memory introduced me to it and I'm afraid I've become rather addicted to it.'

Dodd agreed that the taste, though strong, was delightful and the man chuckled again.

'Another convert, though your conversion will be short lived I'm afraid. There really isn't a lot left in the country.' He stiffened and became much more business-like and Dodd realised that the

45

pleasantries were over and done with. 'Now I'm sure you're wondering why you were told to report here of all places and who I am. Well firstly you may call me Major Smith, and to answer your obvious question that is not my real name or rank, and no I don't work for Mr Selfridge although his store and customers make a perfect cover for me.

He gazed quizzically at Dodd. 'Ah that's got your attention hasn't it? Wondering what you've got yourself into aren't you? Well, we'll get to that later. First tell me about your time in Europe. Take your time. We have all morning and please do not neglect your tea.'

So Dodd began slowly and hesitantly at first but as the Major asked questions he began to enjoy telling the tale. He described his travels and how he had survived and he gave his thoughts on Jorge although the Major seemed more interested in O'Neil, and asked Dodd what he thought of him.

'Well sir he's a clever man and very efficient. We never missed a pick-up and we never thought we were in any danger...but.'

'But?'

'Well sir I only saw him the once you understand but I got the impression that he is very loyal to Jorge and it's his job to protect the General as well as gather information. The Fascists call him the Blue Devil, sir.'

'Really how odd. Isn't blue the colour the Fascists themselves use?'

'It's not that sir, it's his eyes. They are very blue and he always wears a blue shirt simply to annoy the Fascists.'

He paused wondering how to explain a way of life so different to this anonymous office.

'Sir? I heard a tale, I don't know if it's true but Mr Mandel thinks it is and it may tell you more about him and how he thinks.'

'Please go on Sergeant.'

'Well sir it seems that some months ago Franco sent some people to assassinate Jorge but O'Neil's men caught them and they were interviewed personally by O'Neil.'

'Ah a man who takes direct responsibility.'

'Well sir it seems that after the interviews were over O'Neil put them on an aeroplane and parachuted them back over the lines so they could be picked up by the Fascists.'

'That was kind of him, almost chivalrous.'

Dodd shook his head. 'No sir you don't understand, the men were in boxes, lots of small boxes and there was a message that O'Neil had more boxes waiting if Franco wished to try again. I don't know if Franco has tried again but I rather think that O'Neil would like it if they did.'

Strangely the Major did not seem shocked. Indeed Dodd suspected that he approved.

'O'Neil may be extreme sir, but I got the impression that the whole country hates Franco and the Fascists.'

A second cup of tea was poured and the conversation continued. Dodd realised that he was rather skilfully being relieved of every scrap of information he had, and that the Major was judging him, or perhaps had already judged him long before he had taken his first sip of tea.

There were noises in the corridor now as the clerks and secretaries went to lunch and this seemed to animate the major. 'Well Sergeant that's quite a tale you've told me. You are if I may say so a remarkable man. Tell me what are your plans now?'

Dodd was puzzled. He was after all a mere sergeant and sergeants had little chance to form plans. 'Well sir I've re-joined the regiment. We're rather busy now with the new recruits and then there is...' He stopped as he saw the expression on the major's face.

'Training new recruits Sergeant, is I believe a waste of your obvious talents. What if I was able to offer you something better than that?'

A dry chuckle appeared in response to Dodd's obvious interest. 'Ah now you begin to see a little of what this is all about, it is time to lay some of my cards on the table. I belong to an organisation which has been tasked with, as a certain gentleman has put it, *setting Europe alight*. In short, Dodd, we plan to make things rather uncomfortable for Adolph and his cronies. Nothing too big to start with, just a little sabotage, railway tracks, bridges, that sort of thing but most importantly we need to make contact with friendly forces. And you have already done that in Asturias. What if I was to ask you to go back to Spain, oh not right away, but fairly soon, what would you say? There would be a commission in it for you of course.'

'That doesn't matter', thought Dodd as the possibilities opened up in his mind. The Major was right and, though it was odd, he had enjoyed himself on his journey south, and being given the chance to do something similar was very appealing. The decision, he realised, was an easy one to take. 'Thank you, sir. That sounds like something I would like to do.'

'Splendid, your new orders will be along in a few days.'

The interview was obviously over and Dodd had made his bargain. He re-joined the crowds and made his way into the early afternoon air, lost in thought.

It was obviously wrong to believe that the Major and Hugh O'Neill had anything in common. After all the Major was obviously a gentleman while O'Neill was…well whatever he was, he was certainly no gentleman. But all the same, just for a moment as they shook hands and said goodbye he thought he saw O'Neill peeping out of the Major's eyes.

TO SEE A THOUSAND MILES

The voices were wavering, coming and going, rising and falling, never still, always moving. 'We can see. See a thousand miles. Beyond the waves. We can see. Far ahead. A thousand miles. Behind we can see. And on every side. A thousand miles. Or more. All is known, none can hide. We are the radars. A thousand miles. Up or down, we can see. Far or near, we can see. We are the radars, and we can see.'

There was a smattering of applause and loud cheers from her children, though the fifteen inch mouths of her guns contented themselves with half-believing grunts.

She put a welcoming warmth in her voice. 'That was quite an entrance. I am indeed impressed; can you really see a thousand miles?'

There was a short silence followed by an embarrassed series of clicks and hums.

'Well no. But we can see quite far.'   She tried to hide her disappointment.

'How far can you see?'

'Well maybe ten miles...on a good day.'

'Not a thousand miles then.'

'Well no, but we can see aircraft much further away maybe fifty miles, and we can see at night and through cloud and we don't care about fog.'

She tried to hide the excitement in her voice, she feared no ship but aircraft were unsettling.

'You can see aircraft?'

'Oh yes, we can tell how many and how far away.'

'And what if it was just one?'

A little of their pride returned now.

'Oh, one is easy, we can tell you all sorts of things about one aircraft.'

The Hood's malicious chuckle rang through every plate and rivet and her children began to laugh.

The little yellow aircraft flew up and down its sneering voice taunting her. 'Why will you not shoot at me? This is just like last time!'

There was whispering inside her as the radar spoke to the firing computers who in turn spoke to her children who could barely contain their excitement.

'Not a single shot, I can't say I'm surprised. Why waste the ammunition? You know you can't hit me, you really are quite...'

There was a barking roar as her children laughed and a salvo of shells left her. Her nemesis vanished in a hot cloud of burning fabric and half melted steel and then fell writhing into the waiting waves. The Hood let out a great sigh of satisfaction as her children cheered.

'How did we do?' asked the radars.

'Well enough,' she replied. 'And welcome to the Hood.'

An invisible cascade of frigid air had flowed down from the white capped mountains and even a rare winter's sun had failed to banish the cold.

Otto von Stülpnagel's staff tried not to shiver as their general swept the far river bank with his binoculars. The river was a very pretty shade of blue he decided, and the trees had been twisted into pleasing shapes by the wind. He could not know that only a few months earlier a French politician had stood on the same ground and admired the same view. Only the abandoned customs post had changed since then. It now boasted a fresh coat of paint and several military policemen who eyed their general warily.

Von Stülpnagel turned to a fresh-faced man who had newly sewn campaign ribbons on his dress coat. 'So Hans, I wish to cross here. How do I do it?'

Hans smiled, knowing that he was being tested.

'Here General? Why would you wish to cross here? The whole place is a trap, we would all die.'

Stülpnagel laughed. The son of his old friend had not disappointed him.

'Bravo, Hans, bravo. Would you like to tell these gentlemen why we won't be crossing here?'

Hans walked over to a trestle table where a large scale map lay imprisoned under carefully placed rocks. 'We don't cross here because this is where our opponent wishes us to cross. Oh he does not expect us to cross here but he would certainly like us to, of that I am certain. I think I can predict how our battle would go.'

Another map was placed on the table. The second battle of El Mazuco, gentleman. Franco's forces foolishly gave our opponent a whole winter to prepare and he wasted not a second of that time. When he was attacked it was a massacre. He used the ground, the water, the very rocks to kill.'

'And a lot of explosives,' added Stülpnagel.

'Yes General, a lot of explosives but the point I am trying to make is that this man uses what he has to great effect and this valley will be exactly the same. After careful study I believe it is possible to predict the opening moves of our campaign if we cross here. We will throw a bridge across the river and we will take casualties in doing so...but not too many. We will make bridgeheads on the far side and take casualties...but not too many. We will advance along the road and take casualties...but not to many. And when there are enough of us in the valley then the sides of the valley will be blown and we will be trapped and we will die.

'We learn from the mistakes of others, gentlemen. We do not cross here or any other place with a blown bridge. Now maybe this valley is not a trap, and I acknowledge that not every crossing and every valley will be mined but this will be, at least in its initial stage, a mountain campaign where the initiative lies with the defender. No manoeuvring, little in the way of extravagant flanking movements, just a hard series of infantry engagements.'

Hans looked around at the group of men clustered around the windswept table. 'At the general's request I have made a special study of our opponent and the war he wages. I would like to impress on you that this man is dangerous. He seems to have an instinctive grasp of the battlefield, and worse he sees an enemy's weakness before his enemy realises he has made a mistake.'

An impeccably dressed man in a coal black uniform interrupted. 'The Führer has described this man as Aryan in his outlook and Reichsführer Himmler has initiated an investigation into the history of this area. He is convinced that these people are the pure descendants of the Germanic tribes who settled this area in ancient times. That of course is why the Latin races have failed to subdue these people. Naturally in any conflict between an Aryan race and any other, the superior race will subdue the inferior. Reichsführer Himmler has therefore asked me, Herr General, to inform you that if our Führer asks for this operation to be carried out then there are racial aspects which he urges you to consider.

Von Stülpnagel did not allow his emotions to show; Himmler was a growing force in Berlin and the thought of these black-uniformed zealots following his own men filled him with dismay so he placed a false smile on his lips and promised to consider the matter most carefully.

Hans watched his general's diplomatic exchange with interest and decided to take his cue from him. He waited until he was sure that he had everyone's attention once more and then continued, the map still before him. 'After the battle of El Mazuco, a series of lesser, but still important battles took place, notably here at Llanes and at Prado in eastern Asturias. In each one our opponent tricked and deceived his enemies and with each victory he moved east. A seaborne invasion of Asturias was left to capable lieutenants and drowned in a sea of fanatical civilian resistance.'

Stülpnagel shivered, he had heard the tales and had the traditional German fear of Francs-tireurs.

Hans had not noticed his generals shiver and continued. 'But our opponent moved east gentleman and that is important.' He looked expectantly around the table until as he had hoped there was a response.

'Towards France?'

'Towards their rather reluctant sponsor,' agreed Hans, '…but as importantly away from Portugal. And that is important because by not threatening Lisbon the government in Gijón sent an important signal to Prime Minister Salazar and though Portugal does not recognise that Gijón as a legitimate government there have already been low level talks between them. My esteemed colleague from the Reichsführer's office has rightly pointed out the racial aspects of any campaign we may undertake in Spain but the importance of the political dimension cannot be understated. The moment the first field grey uniform crosses the border, suspicions will be aroused in

Portugal and for that matter in Madrid. Both Nations are officially neutral but our relations with Lisbon can best be described as cautiously polite. I imagine that the Führer will give assurances to Lisbon and Madrid but regardless of that our forces must not cross the Asturian or Basque borders into Nationalist territory...not by a single millimetre. Those orders come direct from Berlin and cannot be questioned.

'Also, until certain political matters are arranged, this operation will be carried out entirely by our forces alone. Once we are in control, then things may be different but for now we run our campaign within strict physical and political limits.'

'And just what are those limits Hans?'

'I was coming to that Herr General, if I may continue my little history?'

Von Stülpnagel smiled. 'Tell it your own way Hans.'

'The Nationalist government responded to these victories by moving forces out of North Eastern Spain in order to oppose the forces advancing against them. Not all their forces but enough to give hope to the Basques, some of whom had retreated to mountain hideouts keeping a tiny core of the Republican Basque region alive.

'With far fewer hostile forces to control the area those Basques came down out of the mountains and soon the Nationalists had a bloody guerrilla war behind them. But Franco's generals were still confident. They thought that perhaps the Asturians had by chance found a lucky general but one whose only skill lay in defence. It was an attitude which was to cost them dearly, and if our opponent ever was just a defensive general then he soon learnt the arts of attack. And he learnt them well, so well in fact that at Guernica he took only two days to turn the battle into a Nationalist rout. The rout turned into a bloody, harried retreat and the Nationalists were ejected from the Basque provinces and parts of Northern Navarre. In short we have a nation totally committed to its cause led by a very able commander, and lieutenants who have been in the field for nearly half a decade. And this nation is now, thanks to the government of Leon Blum, in possession of a good deal of expensive weaponry and has received into its army many survivors from the other armies we have recently defeated.

'And let us not deceive ourselves, Asturias is undoubtedly a nation. It stretches from a line a little under one hundred kilometres West of Gijón to the pass at Roncesvalles in the East. Southward the line runs almost parallel with the mountains. Pamplona was taken and Burgos eventually fell to the Asturians. The cities of Leon and Astorga staged popular rebellions and joined Asturias after the fall of Guernica. Reluctantly, and under great pressure the Asturians have divested themselves of the more extreme forms of government and formed an alliance with the Basque Republic as its major ally. The lands around Leon and Astorga are for now being considered autonomous areas. A political compromise was made with the Basques and the Navarrese whereby the Asturians dropped their anti-clericism, again very reluctantly and gave the Navarre conservative factions certain powers and immunities. Despite that there was an exodus of people over the cease fire line which has hurt the Navarrese economy.

'So we have a narrow mountainous land with plains on its northern and southern flanks. This will determine our campaign Her General. They are long flanks and relatively easy to traverse for vehicles.'

'But easy to defend and subject to raids from the mountains, is that not so Hans?'

Hans looked glum. 'Yes Herr General, as I said this will not be an easy campaign.'

A nervous, pale looking man in Luftwaffe uniform spoke. 'Naturally Herr General, the Luftwaffe promises full support and I am sure that there can be no objection made if a request is made to use Fallschirmjäger. I am certain that the Reichsmarschall would be delighted to co- operate with you, if the Führer decides the operation is to go ahead.'

Von Stülpnagel looked coldly at the nervous man. Göering's star had somewhat dimmed after his failure to subdue the Royal Airforce and this campaign would be seen as a chance to replace some of that lost lustre. And that was a game he was not going to play, this would be an Army affair and the army would determine just how the Luftwaffe would contribute.

The man began to wilt under his stare and began to stammer out some nonsense or other but von Stülpnagel held up his hand and the words ground to a halt. 'Thank you, I will expect a full report on my desk by the end of the week, and I want to see facts not fantasies. Please continue Hans.'

'Thank you, Herr General. As I was saying if we follow just one route then we allow our opponent to concentrate against us .Follow both flanks and we have the mountains between us, dividing our forces and leaving us potentially at the end of very long fragile supply lines. I therefore suggest we supply our northern flank by sea. That way we could bypass these damned mountains.

'Not going to happen.' The reply came from a man with a scarred face where one bloodshot eye stared rigidly and blindly to one side.

Stülpnagel knew that he had commanded a turret on the Scharnhorst in its fight with the Hood. The Scharnhorst had survived...barely but had been badly damaged. The Kreigsmarine had patched the man up and given him a staff job. The seaman had the virtue of being blunt but never gave anything other than an honest opinion.

'We don't have the assets to do so,' the man continued. 'U-boats and a few Schnellboots maybe; enough to overcome local naval forces but as for larger units?' He shook his head. 'Out of the question. We lost too many in Norway and I think my superiors would be reluctant to risk moving our remaining heavy units down here. And any commercial shipping would have to come from shipping presently in the French ports we now own, and that impacts on our treaty with Vichy. How you cut that knot is for people with more gold braid on their arms than I have.'

He touched a sleeve which held a hand covered in pink scar tissue and looked sadly at von Stülpnagel. 'Then there's a lot of neutral shipping around - Swedish, American, all sorts. That complicates things a little. I can ask, but please don't get your hopes up.'

He paused and scratched a half healed face. 'And then there's the monster you don't want to think about.' A scarred grin had appeared on the man's face at the sight of a group of puzzled faces. 'The British, Herr General, the British. We cross over that border and move along your Lieutenants' coast road and you think the Royal Navy will just roll over in their bunks and go back to sleep? Not a chance in hell, General. A couple of their cruisers, half a dozen destroyers and it's goodbye shipping, and goodbye Schnellboot's and any U-Boot will be damn careful before it pops its head up.'

Von Stülpnagel nodded. This was as he had expected but Hans was appalled.

'They would lose ships also', Hans countered, 'surely that would make them think twice before moving precious ships down here.'

'And we also would also take a toll on them.' added the Luftwaffe officer.

'All true,' agreed the scarred man. 'I'm sure they would lose ships but how much comfort would that be to you when you run out of ammunition because your supply ship never made it to shore? Oh and if you think that's bad, try advancing along a coast road with an enemy cruiser laying its guns on you.'

He turned to von Stülpnagel. 'I'm sorry Herr General, truly I am and I will ask my superiors to give all the help they can but for the Kreigsmarine this operation would be suicide and pointless suicide at that.'

The air was getting colder now, and a bitter wind was doing its best to lift the maps from the table. Von Stülpnagel looked up. The sun was resting on the top of the mountains and casting pink and black shadows on the group who were beginning to shiver a little more. He decided to take pity on them and draw this little meeting to a close. He turned to a cold and unhappy looking Hans.

'Well it is not a pretty picture you have painted for us this afternoon. An able and experienced general with able and experienced lieutenants operating from interior lines supported by a fanatical populace who will hate our guts from the moment we cross the border. We have to cross these mountains, and once we do we are forced by military and political considerations to advance down a single corridor where every man with a rifle will try and kill us. Have I missed anything Hans?'

Hans looked even more unhappy. 'I think you have very ably summarised the problems Herr General.'

'Don't look so sad Hans. Did I not tell you that this would be very different to riding on a Panzer? You have performed the first of your duties admirably, now comes the difficult part.'

'The difficult part Herr General?'

'Why yes, now you have to find solutions to all those problems.'

The laughter did much to relieve the mood among his staff and as the last of the light fled from night's unwelcome advances von Stülpnagel walked to the water's edge and looked over to the far bank. *It would be a shame,* he thought, *to desecrate such a scene with the blood of many men but that was war and he was a soldier, and if he was honest he already had the blood of many men on his hands.*

He never spotted the two men watching him.

'Kill him!'

The voice was soft, but insistent. 'Kill him. You have the Englishman's rifle, kill him!'

Jorge sighted along the rifle and the man's head appeared to be at the end of the barrel. Truly it was a marvellous weapon Dodd had given him. Even at this distance the man's life was in his hands.

'Kill him!' the voice was in his ear now, still soft and still insistent. A little more pressure on the trigger, just a little more and the man's head would explode into ribbons of pink and grey.

"I can't carry this with me',' Dodd had said, "will you take it please?"

He had lusted after the rifle since he had first held it and now he had the proven killer in his hands.

'Kill him, kill the German general!'

The voice was a little louder now but Jorge refused to obey and lowered the rifle. 'Not today Hugh, not today.'

Hugh O'Neil's blue eyes blazed for a while then lost a little of their glitter as sanity clawed its way back into his mind. He gave a low laugh. 'Perhaps you are right, perhaps it is better to kill many rather than one but that was Stülpnagel, the General the arch Fascist has placed in charge of France. 'Kill him and you hurt them.'

Jorge shook his head. 'Hitler has many generals, Hugh. He has more generals than my brother had sheep. If I kill this one, another two arrive, and I have lost because now they have a cause to attack.'

Hugh growled his dissent. 'They do not need an excuse my General. Did I not tell you that he would be here today and why? I have many friends over the border and they have told me why those bastards are here today.'

'I never doubted your word Hugh. They will come in the spring perhaps when the snow has gone.'

'Up this valley?'

O'Neil's voice was hopeful. He knew the traps that lay in wait for the unwary and for a moment delicious visions of mangled limbs and crushed skulls danced before his eyes.

'No Hugh, though I would like him to do so. Have you not told me he is a man of experience, a clever man? And that is good. I limit his options, and better I sow a little doubt in his mind. I use his knowledge and his own mind against him. A stupid man would blunder in but this man will think and plan. He will say: *Shall I pick this valley or this one? Perhaps this is the road that is mined...or is it this one?*'

Jorge smiled at his friend. 'There are few roads and many valleys. So he will hesitate and that gives us time.'

O'Neil tried to hide his disappointment. 'And once he crosses the mountains what then?'

The smile vanished and Jorge's shoulders shrugged in resignation.

'Then Hugh we have another war to wage. The Basques will harry him until he hits the plains. They will give him no peace and we will give him no peace. We wait to see what choices he makes, and we hope.'

The Germans were leaving now, a long snake of black cars winding up through the snow-laden trees, and for a moment he envied their passengers, secure in their heated interiors. He sighed as he realised that even if Asturias had such cars the petrol to run such extravagances did not exist and that peasants, even peasant generals had been given legs for such occasions as this.

He rose and began to brush the snow from his coat and as he did so an old memory sprang into his mind. 'I don't have a magic mirror Hugh, I wish I did.' He smiled at Hugh's obvious puzzlement. 'An old tale of my grandmother's she told of an English sailor who fought King Phillipe a long time ago. It was said that he had a magic mirror which foretold the movements of every Spanish ship. For a thousand miles no Spanish ship was safe.'

O'Neil was dismissive, 'A tale for children.'

'Yes Hugh, a tale for children but in truth I wish I had such a mirror.'

They began to walk back now, careful to avoid the paths that had the hidden wires and the cunningly poised rocks.

'If I had such a mirror then all the generals and all the soldiers in the world could not prevail against us.'

O'Neil gave a rare smile, hoping to dispel his general's mood.

'I am your mirror my General. I will seek out their secrets....and if I fail?' Jorge looked up expectantly. 'Why then you have the Englishman's magic rifle!'

A WORD FROM OUR SPONSORS

'This is H.V Kaltenborn reading the news. A near riot took place this morning at a bookshop in New York where the celebrated author Martha Gelhorn was signing copies of her new bestseller *No Need For Fame*. It seems that some of her many fans clashed with a street demonstration involving men wearing Nazi arm bands and bearing placards denouncing the author as a communist. Gellhorn's book which has risen rapidly to top the best sellers list is a searing account of the war in Northern Spain and has evoked sympathy in many and anger in others. Police are investigating and several arrests were made.

'In other news the German Foreign Ministry today announced the leader of Nationalist Spain, General Francisco Franco, has been invited to a summit at the German Chancellor's mountain retreat in Austria. Also believed to be attending is the Italian dictator, Benito Mussolini. No word has been received as to the subject of the talks and sources close to Madrid will say only that the General will be attending. What this means for the war in its second year we can only guess and what the response here in Washington will be...'

Cordell Hull reached out an elegant hand and Kaltenborn's voice softened into a background mumble. He turned and faced the man who sat behind the ornate desk. 'Well Mr President, you heard Kaltenborn. Just what are we going to do?'

The trademark grin appeared and a long stream of smoke was pulled down the cigarette holder. 'About the book? Already got one thanks.' He held up a new but already well-thumbed copy of Gellhorn's book. A small girl smiled out from the dust cover, a doll in one hand and a very small piece of bread in the other.

Hull sighed, he had his own copy.

'If only you could take my wife's copy, she's joined one of those Bundles for Bilbao committees. Our house is filled with women sorting out donated clothing and dolls... Dolls, Mr President....Dolls. I think every girl in America has donated a damn doll and if even half of them arrive every child in Northern Spain will have a doll. A man can't get any peace in his own house for chattering women and second-hand clothes.' The grin broadened as the cigarette smoke was expelled.

'What do you expect? We're a generous people. Gelhorn has a best seller and people have a cause they can feel happy about.' Hull shook his head.

"Write your Congressman!' The grin looked a little less assured now and the cigarette smoke weakened. Gellhorn had ended her book with an appeal for help for the Asturians and a request that her readers enlist the aid of their elected representatives.

'It's not a flood Mr President, not yet but I've had a few visits to my office mentioning that these letters are hitting desks.

Roosevelt nodded. Hull was an important link between him and Capitol Hill.

'It may be a flash in the pan Mr President but then again it may not be. There are still plenty of letters insisting that we stay out of the war but a little less of them every day. The question is Mr President, will you include the Asturians in your speech next week? Will you promise them aid? You know what that conference in Austria is about. You know Hitler will pressure Franco to join the Axis powers. We've both seen those reports the British have sent. Even if Franco resists Hitler's invitation, Germany is capable of crossing the Pyrenees without Spanish help and if that happens, then God help the Asturians. The British estimate that inside of four months the Basques and the Asturians will be forced back into the mountains. And if the Germans do force the passes and gain victory then they gain more bases from which to attack the Atlantic convoys and they'll be in a position to strike south towards Gibraltar with or without Franco's permission.

'And regardless of whether they move south or not they will certainly take for themselves the iron and potash that the British now take from Spain and the wolfram ore that the War department keeps telling us is vital in keeping Germany supplied with everything from armour plate to machine tools. At the moment the Germans have been using their reserve stocks and importing wolfram from Sweden but that's an unsatisfactory solution as far as they are concerned.

'Spain and Portugal are Germany's main suppliers but with the Asturians holding the main roads and rail lines that lead into German controlled France, every ton of ore takes weeks to get over the border. It's not a situation that Berlin will allow to drag on too long, Mr President. The British have been buying up every ton of wolfram they can, and pressuring Portugal to limit their exports but they're reaching the limits of what they can do and if Germany does invade then they will have to intervene.'

Roosevelt's cigarette had died and his hands were busy fixing a new one into the still warm holder. The phone between London and his office had been in constant use these past few days. Churchill had been adamant that if Spain was invaded they would recognise the Asturians and the Basques as free nations and send forces to help them, even if that meant using resources earmarked for their Far East possessions.

Churchill had even talked to that new Frenchman, Mandel, who had somehow escaped from France and travelled extensively through northern Spain It had been a fascinating talk and the Frenchman had several interesting ideas but none that helped him here and now.

The cigarette flared into life and Roosevelt looked up at Hull. 'All that you say is true Mr Secretary and I will tell the American people that we must, for our own protection, give material aid to those democracies still fighting against Fascism but how do we give aid to people we don't recognise as a nation? As I understand it these people have no recognised currency, nothing in the way of dollar holdings and their economy, based on steel and coal with farming and fishing, desperately needs rebuilding. If I give the Asturians so much as a new bicycle, Congress will hand me my ass on a platter and you know it.

'I imagine the Asturians could do much with a few tanks and a couple of squadrons of bombers but without money my hands are tied.'

The radio continued in the background as the two men pondered the question.

Hull looked at his president for a few moments and then softly spoke a single word. 'Finland.'

Roosevelt looked puzzled wondering what connection a small nation bordering the Arctic circle could have with a fledgling country bordering the Atlantic Ocean.

'Finland?'

'Finland Mr President. Last winter Congress passed a bill allowing the Import-Export bank you set up to loan money to the Finnish reconstruction bank to aid in repairing the damage done in their war with the Soviets.'

Roosevelt's cigarette died un- noticed as he listened to Hull.

'Only subsequent amendments to the bill mentioned Finland but the original bill does not, and it gives discretion to loan up to twenty million so long as it does not break the Neutrality Act. Twenty million buys a lot of tractors and cement Mr President.

Roosevelt was beginning to see the possibilities.

'Finland?'

'Yes, that's our entry point, Mr President. We'll channel the money through the British or possibly ask them to help the Asturians set up their own recovery bank like the Finns. We can claim that the loan is for humanitarian purposes only.'

'But how do the Asturians pay the loan back Cordell? They have no cash. Their paper money is worthless outside of their borders.' He shook his head. 'Congress will raise hell if we announce this.'

Cordell's wintery smile was not designed to light up the room but Roosevelt saw it and knew that there was an answer.

'Not so Mr President, in fact...' He paused for a moment, listening, and then turned to the radio.

A moment later the voice echoed from the walls. "And that was the news sponsored by the Socony-Vacuum Oil Company. Always use Socony-Vacuum Oil in your car. No other oil gives more protection to your engine. Remember you can be sure with Socony."

The radio was once more muted and Hull turned back towards the ornate desk.

'That's how we do it Mr President. We find the Asturians sponsors - American companies that will invest in their mines and factories. We will deny that this is an acknowledgement of Asturian sovereignty and insist that this is merely a humanitarian loan and American business men looking for new opportunities. This way the Asturians will gain a little cash, the Germans will maybe have second thoughts or at least delay their invasion now we've taken an interest. It's not much but it's as much as we can do right now. Get hold of Churchill, ask him to contact the Asturians and tell them if they are open for business we are too.'

Roosevelt grimaced, his mind full of the problems this policy would surely cause in Congress.

'And Franco Mr Secretary? This action may just drive him into the arms of the Axis powers.'

'It may Mr President but he's had a taste of what happens when he veers a little too close to Berlin and Rome. The last time he did that we cut off his oil supplies and the Canadians stopped sending him wheat. I doubt he wants a repeat of that. No, I recommend we carry on exporting oil and wheat and maintain normal relations with Madrid. The wheat and the oil and the exports to Britain will be a constant reminder of what they have to gain by staying neutral. Franco knows that if Germany does invade he'll never get Asturias back and instead of having a strong aggressive neighbour over the Pyrenees he'll have a strong aggressive neighbour in the next field. We need to convince him that a Northern Spain, able to resist Hitler is his best option right now. If Franco is smart he'll stall for time, cloud the issue. It buys us time also Mr President, public opinion is swinging our way and your speech will help that process. I've already started making calls, Mr President. We can start the process at any time you want.'

Roosevelt glanced at the bank of phones which lay on his desk, picked one up and spoke, 'Mabel? What time is it in London? 'It is, is it?

'Put me through anyway.'

There was a pause and the silence in the room fought with muted dance music. At last a growling voice came over the speakers.

'Winston? Sorry to wake you. I've got Cordell Hull in the room with me. He's got an idea. It's risky but it might help with that Asturian situation we were discussing last week.'

He handed the phone over to Hull with a grin. 'Your ball Mr Secretary, your ball.'

The measured tick of the clock and the chatter of men and typewriters were a constant background noise but Hull's voice was clear enough as Churchill listened to the words that fought their way down the long cable.

'That sounds as if it may cause some degree of anger within your Congress, Mr Secretary but I imagine that you know how to manage your own house best. Your bank, not to mention your investors, may be taking a considerable risk.'

There was a pause as his comment was answered.

'No it is certainly better than nothing and as you say this action may cause a small degree of trepidation in Berlin. Of course the money is a secondary consideration but I would caution you that Herr Hitler is persuaded by one thing and one thing only and an action like this, though welcome will weigh lightly in the balance if he decides that the might of Germany is to be thrown across the Pyrenees.'

'An Asturian bank Mr Secretary?' He stopped and considered for a moment. 'The Asturians have no banking system to speak of so perhaps a bank based in a neutral country would be better but the details can be arranged later. Better for now to agree and let other days solve those problems.'

'Nothing could be simpler, I have but to pick up a phone and the matter is settled. We are, as you know, in constant contact with Gijón and Monsieur Mandel has been most assiduous in promoting their cause.'

'Oh you've seen the reports? Then you will have seen his agreement that nothing precipitate should be done at this stage.'

'Yes by all means continue supplying oil. I will prevail upon Premier Mackenzie King to assure Franco that Canadian wheat will continue to flow.'

'No I agree, nothing should be done to alarm Madrid, but they must be forced into the realisation that not only do they not have the means to retake Northern Spain but at this point in time they are better off with an Asturias which we regard with friendly eyes, rather than a whole Spain which could only be regarded with suspicion.

The next comment brought forth a short lived smile.

'Yes Mr Secretary, our lives would be much simpler if Franco had conquered all of Spain but we have to live in the world as it is, not as we would wish it to be. The Asturians are a fact, and though I deplore their politics they have surely earned the right to be heard. And from a purely practical viewpoint we cannot allow Hitler access to any more of Europe's coastline.'

'Ah yes I do agree. No I don't think so. If Franco is wise…if he is careful…if he is cautious, he will remain as still as the mouse that hears the claw click of the cat. My fear is that that no amount of care, no superfluity of caution will stop that particular cat from pouncing.'

The telephone line then delivered a question that had haunted him for weeks.

'I have no idea if Franco will resist a crossing of the border Mr Secretary. Certainly there are those within Spain who would welcome closer ties with the Axis powers. Then again Spanish national pride is no inconsiderable force and we may yet see Spain once more plunged into fratricidal strife. The matter is very uncertain indeed. My earnest hope is that Franco will be able to resist the blandishments of those who would welcome Nazi jackboots. But I must make it plain to you, that in the event of Nazi aggression we will be forced to act. We have made our position very clear. His Majesty's forces will strike and strike very hard indeed, Mr Secretary, the moment the first Nazi crosses the border. Plans already formed will be enacted. Regardless of the consequences, regardless of the cost, regardless of the losses we would undoubtedly suffer…we will strike.'

There was concern in the next questions.

'Well that can't be helped. An immediate danger is, I am sure you will agree, far more pressing than a danger which may never happen, and if by some mischance Japan does strike some time will elapse before our possessions come under absolute threat and of course we have Singapore just as you have your magnificent base on Hawaii, both impregnable bastions which can withstand any attack.'

'Well that's the best we can do. I cannot defend these islands, hold onto the Middle East, remain ready to strike at Spain and at the same time reinforce the Far East. I'm sorry but the forces at our command are far from infinite.'

'Yes I'm sorry too, I'm glad you understand.'

He hoped they did understand and was glad when the next question was one he found more agreeable.'

'Yes, Mr Secretary. I have sent Prime Minister Salazar assurances of our good will and promises of support should the worst happen. He is of course in a difficult position. He despises German imperial ambitions, yet rightly fears the spread of the war. There are plans in place to evacuate his government to the Azores should Portugal be overrun.'

'An invasion of Spain would, if handled properly have most useful consequences for us if Lisbon could be persuaded to exchange her present neutrality into something more belligerent.'

The telephone was growing hot against his ear and he shifted uneasily on the hard chair as the next question flowed from Hull.

'I think there is very little chance of that Mr Secretary. Gijón has been most attentive in allaying Senor Salazar's fears along those lines and has steadfastly refused to attempt to move her borders west, even when she could, even when it would have been highly gratifying for her to do so. There has as you know been some amount of discussion between the two capitals. Nothing at a very high level to be sure but enough so that in the event of invasion Salazar would consider Asturias to be an ally, though most certainly not a friend.'

The telephone crackled for a moment distorting the words, but enough of them got through to make the next question clear. He could appreciate the idea and now was not the time to disagree outright. 'That is stretching a very long bow indeed Mr Secretary. I'm sure that President Monroe never considered the Azores to be covered under his famous doctrine but under certain circumstances, and if you were to give Lisbon very firm assurances indeed then possibly we might not object if the United States was to stretch out its powerful hand in that area.

He chuckled at the next question. 'It may be that he does, indeed I expect he will certainly try but please remember that the flower of Italian youth lie dead in North Africa or languish behind wire guarded by his Majesty's troops. Mussolini may yet rue the day that he threw in his lot with Hitler and certainly we shall waste no opportunity to bring the Duce to his knees. The prudent course for Mussolini would be to cheer from the side-lines but I fear that pride and stupidity may whisper louder in the ears of the man than the voices of wise council and we may yet see the Italian fleet sally out.'

'No, Mr Secretary I'm not at all sure he can do both. Certainly an Italian expeditionary force to Eastern Spain would as you say come at the cost of reducing supplies to Libya. Naturally in that event certain opportunities arise for us that you may be sure we will take full advantage of.'

The laughter came clearly down the line.

'Yes that is a pleasing thought isn't it? Was there anything else Mr Secretary?'

'Very well, the arrangements for the Asturian bank will be put in train. Goodnight Mr Secretary.'

He placed the telephone back in its cradle and sat for a moment lost in thought. The Americans were becoming more involved in the war and the Roosevelt administration was obviously trying to position itself so that when it took its place in the ranks of those fighting the Axis it would possess several advantages.

On the one hand whilst most gratifying it clouded the future more than he would like. An America cured of isolationism could be most troublesome. That though was a matter for another day. Today's first task was one that gave him a good deal of personal satisfaction.

He looked up at the clock.

There was still time for a leisurely breakfast.

There was still a little egg on Churchill's face which Mandel was doing his best to ignore but at last the dishes were pushed away and a cup of tea was placed before him. He had never understood the British obsession with having huge breakfasts. A breakfast should be a light repast, an overture to lunch, something which delighted the palate but did not overload the stomach. He looked at the brown sludge which masqueraded as tea and pushed it away with a little shiver of distaste. To his vast relief a napkin removed the last evidence of the eggs existence and Churchill smiled.

'I have only just become used to you Georges. It seems a pity to lose you so soon.'

'It's only a month Prime Minister. The time will go quickly.'

'And God willing, Georges, profitably You are sure this is the only way?'

'Perhaps not the only way but certainly the quickest way and possibly the best. I need to be seen and in places other than London. There are power centres other than here, places where other Frenchmen live. So I must travel and borrow power before I pounce and remove

De Gaulle. I must at the very least nurture the doubts that exist about him.

'Alas on my first visit to the United States I will appear not as Georges Mandel but as a cypher, a ghost, an all too deniable vestige of the France that was. Doors will be opened to me but no records will be kept. No journalist will beg for an interview. My bed will be in a back room in a third rate hotel. I will speak not to those who hold power but only to those who have the ears of those who hold power.'

He saw that Churchill was about to speak and moved quickly to defuse the acid response liable to burst from angry lips. 'My dear Mr Churchill, please do not think that I am ungrateful. You have been my true and faithful herald. Without you those doors would have remained closed. And I can assure you that for a chance such as this I would spend a lifetime in such a hotel...even if it served tea such as this.

Churchill's angry reply died before it could leap over his teeth and embed itself in Mandel's body. Instead a half rueful smile appeared. He had grown to like this Frenchman with his dry wit and implacable hatred of Fascism. 'I've done what I can,' he said. 'The rest is up to you.'

A great sigh escaped him. 'You won't be able to change their minds you know. Washington is convinced that France is still a potential ally, that given the right encouragement she will rise up against her captors.

Mandel nodded. There were no hills before him, but mountains. *Still,* he thought, *it would not be the first time I've had to climb mountains.* 'And we both know that they will not,' he replied. 'De Gaulle sends messages to an empty room. The France he and I knew no longer exists, it died six long months ago. De Gaulle wishes France renewed. I on the other hand wish to see France reborn. The Americans cannot see that Vichy is the corpse of an old man, they see France through eyes that are fixed on past glories and past achievements.'

Churchill shook his head. 'They will not be parted from Vichy, Georges. God knows I've tried.'

Mandel's smile rose up like a bubble in a champagne flute. 'My dear Prime Minister, I do not seek to divorce Washington from Vichy.

Time alone will do that. What I need to do is divorce you from De Gaulle.'

Mandel's grin now had an answering echo on Churchill's face.

'I would be a most willing divorcee.'

'As I suspected, Prime Minister, as I suspected. A marriage of convenience has its limitations does it not?'

'And you expect me to leap into your arms, Georges? Perhaps I would be better off as a single man.'

Mandel's grin swiftly changed into a dry laugh. 'Nonsense, you need France but you need a France that sees that the old days are gone for ever. Appeals to glory are useless, worse than useless. In fact, they are a waste of effort and precious, precious time. De Gaulle speaks to France but who is listening? Very few I imagine. Certainly, too few to matter and what is worse, none that do matter. How many French soldiers rescued at such great cost simply returned home, exchanging freedom for captivity? Too many, Prime Minister, and those that remain are not enough to give power to my voice.

'I need to convince others that when Vichy fails, as fail she will, that there are Frenchmen who opened their hands in Friendship. Long before that I intend to gnaw away at De Gaulle.' A bitter smile was not a normal part of Mandel's repertoire, but he managed to produce one. 'I offered De Gaulle my hand. I offered him advice and counsel, I offered him much but he spurned me, so now he will pay.'

Churchill grunted. He was seeing Mandel's hard core exposed. Rescuing the man from Spain was proving to have been a wise decision. As he suspected, Mandel and De Gaulle had from their first meeting hated each other.

'At least you have stolen a march on him by forming a French government in exile. De Gaulle was in the process of forming one, but you have stolen more than one good man away from him.'

The bitter smile grew a little harder. 'And I intend to steal many more from him. Am I not seen with you? Are De Gaulle's broadcasts not curtailed? Men can see which way the tree is leaning and they do not wish to be under it when it falls.'

The pleasant smile returned and Mandel's body lost its angry rigidity, relaxing into a more comfortable stance. 'But please do not fall into the trap of calling my group a government. You and I both know that the Americans at least would not recognise it as such. No, what I have formed is an association of Frenchmen who are interested in politics and the war. If others see us as a government in exile, then that cannot be helped but we do not call ourselves a government....for now.

'But Washington, while it does not wish to enrage Vichy, is intrigued or are at least so curious about my ideas that they wish to see me and that my dear Churchill, is enough....for now. Perhaps I will make such a good impression that the Americans, will ask you to form ever closer ties with me as a possible counter to Vichy, if I can convince them that there is a France that will not only fight, but fight with common goals. So yes, Prime Minister, I intend to marry you as you so delicately put it. I will not be your dog. I serve France before all others, but your friendship – that I value highly. Together we will prise those grubby German hands off the throat of France and then we will walk together in amity.'

There was a grunt of approval from the other side of the table and a post breakfast cigar was lit. "Hands off indeed, Georges. And may that day come soon but I fear that many hard days and no few tears lie between us and that happy event. I have arranged berths for you on H.M.S King George the Fifth, you will...'

He stopped on seeing the blood drain from Mandel's face. 'Is there something wrong Georges? Your cabin will be quite comfortable I assure you.'

Mandel was struggling to find words to express his emotions. 'You expect me to travel with that collaborationist......that traitor?'

For a moment a memory of a painful interview passed through Churchill's mind, of pale skin stretched tightly over a high-domed forehead and the bland sphinx-like expression which was all that Lord Halifax had given him on receiving the news that he was being ejected from the cabinet and being sent to America as ambassador.

Given Mandel's recent history and indomitable spirit it was perfectly natural that the thought of travelling with Halifax would fill him with horror. He tried to pacify the now very angry Frenchman. 'Georges please try and calm yourself. I had no intention of you travelling with, or even meeting Lord Halifax. A battleship is a very big ship and the crew will be under strict instructions that your presence on board is to be considered an absolute secret, even from Lord Halifax and his party. As you say your visit to America is to remain confidential and that secrecy manifests itself at all times, both before and after. You need have no fears that you will so much as lay eyes on anyone but the crew. Indeed it is my intention to visit the ship to impress upon the crew the necessity of you remaining a secret while on board.'

A hesitant smile fought its way through Mandel's indignation. 'Thank you Prime Minister. I understand the necessity of you continuing to use Lord Halifax, but the thought of...'

'We will say no more of it, Georges. I wish you good luck and please remember that not only are you your own ambassador in America, but to a certain extent, albeit in a limited fashion, mine also. Speak strong words but softly is my advice, and now since it seems you have no intention of drinking my tea, perhaps it would be as well if you began your preparations.'

It was a polite dismissal and a mollified and excited Mandel left Churchill alone with his thoughts. A France free of German hands was undoubtedly a good thing but there was a greater danger. Greater American involvement in the war was desirable, even necessary but with that greater involvement would come a wish to participate in decisions in which they had no practical experience. And how to keep Washington's hands off the direction of the war was a problem without an answer, at least none that he could presently see.

He sighed and turned to the vivid red folder marked *Alacrity*.

Alacrity, the code word for the British invasion of Northern Spain.

An invasion which looked ever more probable

LIGHTING THE FUSE

The single good eye of the sailor stared at Hans and the crooked mouth smiled. 'It's a good plan as far as it goes, and it ought to work, God knows we've put enough effort into it. We boot the door in and keep moving as fast as we can, the Luftwaffe clears the way and we move along clearly defined paths. While my lot,' he touched the dark navy-blue uniform, 'do their best to draw off the Royal Navy and lie in wait of the Spanish coast.'

Hans smiled and gently contradicted the scarred man. 'We move only as fast as the enemy will let us.'

The crooked smile vanished. 'Which enemy Hans? The Basques? The Asturians? The British? And if we do go ahead without Franco agreeing perhaps the Spanish and Portuguese? And what then, Hans? The Americans? The Russians? We seem to be acquiring enemies the same way my dog acquires fleas.'

Hans looked around nervously. Such talk was verging on disloyalty. They were alone in the room but even so the words were dangerous.

'Be careful my friend, the walls are thin here.' He gestured across the room to where the black uniforms lay.

A hand covered in angry red skin waved dismissively. 'Chocolate soldiers every one of them. Mere strutting cockerels who sit on their dunghills and crow nonsense that others believe. You and I have seen war, we know what it is like.'

He gestured at the thick folders and detailed maps.

'Those damn things are going to kill people; we know it, and we regret it but we do it because we are soldiers and we obey orders. But those people? They would not care if every blue jacket and every field grey uniform was lost forever so long as they could continue to preach.'

He looked at the growing alarm on Hans face.

'All right my friend; I too will cease preaching. Besides it's too late now. Your general has approved our plans and copies are no doubt sitting on the Führer's desk as we speak. It's just a shame that the Asturians and the Basques will suffer because of something that Franco did.'

Hans nodded. 'Surely it's something he didn't do. If he had conquered all of Spain then we would not have to invade to secure those mines.'

The sailors laugh had only a little scorn in it. 'Hans, Hans. You really are a soldier aren't you. If it doesn't have wheels, tracks or hooves you just don't care. Don't you read your own reports? The whole Asturian Republic is Franco's fault or at least his navy's fault. Way back in '38, the Nationalist Navy was chasing a British flagged blockade runner. A Royal Navy Destroyer got in the way and was hit pretty badly. So badly in fact its captain decided to make repairs in the nearest port - which happened to be Gijón. Somehow, and I suspect our opponents' devious hand here, a rumour started that the destroyer was the lead ship of a British intervention. Franco panicked and withdrew giving the Asturians precious time. Time they used to gain victories and to persuade the French that they could survive. You may not have noticed but I assure you that we of the Kreigsmarine took a very great interest in the matter. The captain was very nearly cashiered as I recall.'

He steepled his fingers together and looked over them at Hans. 'Now just suppose that the British had a heavy unit on hand to support the destroyer - heavy cruiser or something a little bigger even - do you think the Spanish captain would have been bold enough to open fire? Of course not. The whole matter would have played out very differently I expect. Franco would have continued his conquests, and we would not be planning to invade Spain to access an ore that I was in happy ignorance of until a few months ago.'

The crooked smile returned.

'So you see Hans all this is Franco's fault ...or possibly the Royal Navy's.'

Hans laughed at this flight of fancy, the sailor had a keen mind and was not lacking in imagination but this was a little too much to be a convincing argument. 'We must live in the real world. The Asturians are a fact, our lack of tungsten is a fact and these plans will give us both. We have done our duty and now the matter is out of our hands.'

A scarred hand gestured towards the office that housed the carefully tailored black uniforms.

'And their hands, Hans, do not forget those hands.

The last of the carefully hoarded Lapsang Souchong was now just a memory and today his cup contained tea from a packet which gaudily proclaimed its allegiance to the Republic of China. He rather suspected that the tea had been no nearer China than a warehouse in Bombay but that was only to be expected after over a year of war.

'We all have to make sacrifices' he thought sardonically, stirring yesterday's milk into today's brew. A life time of stern denial easily overcame an instinctive grimace of distaste as the first of the tea insulted his taste buds. Only a knock on the door saved him from further regrets over the fortunes of war.

A smiling man entered, brown-stained teeth and yellow-stained fingers witnessed his addiction to tobacco, while a certain redness in his face indicated another more serious habit. Despite that or possibly because of it the man was a most valuable asset so the smile was returned while the tea was rejected.

'Ah home is the hunter. Welcome back, Fleming. I trust that that all went well?'

'Better than I'd hoped, sir. The Asturians now have a bank with rather less than twenty million United States dollars in it.'

'Rather less?'

A cigarette flared into brief life.

'Rather less sir. Setting up the bank was easy, family connections you know.'

The Major nodded, Fleming's family had been merchant bankers for generations. 'And why Uruguay, Fleming? Surely there are closer places.'

A smile peeped out behind the cigarette smoke and the points were ticked off on stained fingers. 'Several reasons sir.

'Firstly, the Asturians just don't have the expertise to run banks. They are after all communists, or at least former communists. Oh, they have a lot of economic theories but no practical experience of running a trading bank. I mean look at their paper currency; it really is a mess. So, for now sir, an off-shore bank, which brings me to my next reason.

75

'It seems a few American Congressmen have got wind of the loan, so I thought it would be best for all concerned if we made it as difficult as possible for those gentlemen to pry into the affairs of what is now a wholly foreign owned bank.'

Fleming's second cigarette burst into life.

'Lots of British ex pats down there, sir, every one of them wanting to do their bit for the old country. Lots of ranchers, mine owners that sort of thing, and enough bankers to make the job simple. The language of course helps tremendously, and then there are the banking rules down there. They can be a little...elastic. For a very reasonable price I was able to speed things up quite a bit and El Banco de Reconstrucción Norte now has a suitably small office in a back street in Montevideo and several million dollars to its name.'

'Several, Fleming?' You have been busy.'

'No rest for the wicked, Major. You know that.'

A sad smile flickered like summer lightening on the Major's face. 'More than most,' he replied, 'more than most. Do please continue.'

'Thank you, sir, as I was saying, I then flew back to America where I've set up the trading arm of our new bank. *Universal Exports* is now up and running from an obscure postal address in rural Wyoming. I've put one of our chaps in charge of it and to do the fellow credit he hasn't been idle. He managed to pick up a job lot of tractors and earth movers in Texas and they're already on their way to Asturias.'

'Well I'm certain that they will be most useful, Fleming. After all there is a lot of work for that sort of equipment over there.'

Fleming's laugh broke through the Major's carefully cultivated exterior. A deep frown appeared on his face. His war was a serious one and although Fleming was an excellent operator there were limits to his patience.

Fleming continued before the rebuke could be uttered. 'I'm sure that they would be most useful if the Asturians were going to use them as tractors but we picked them for their engines, rather than any use they may have in urban renewal. You see sir, I ran across an odd chap called Higgins, and it seems he has an idea for fast wooden patrol craft...and well sir, we got to talking.'

'In a bar I suppose.' The major had no use for alcohol. Tea was his vice and it seemed as if even fell inevitably to be curtailed.

'Well yes, sir, as it happens in a bar but the upshot is that two of his craft are now deck cargo on the ship with the tractors and the Asturians have a licence to build them.

'Not as patrol boats surely.'

'Oh no, sir. The plans say that they are fishing boats.'

'And the tractor engines are placed in the torpedo boats I suppose.'

'Yes, sir. The Asturians already have torpedoes supplied by the French last summer. They were going to place them along the shore line but I thought this was a better use for them.'

'It seems you exceeded your authority a little, Fleming.'

The man looked suitably abashed. 'It seemed a good idea at the time sir.'

The Major could easily imagine the scene; a bar, a plausible salesman and the bargain being struck. 'No doubt,' he said dryly. 'Well there's no use crying over spilt milk. I only hope that no one finds out until it's too late. Now fuel, Fleming; petrol, oils, that sort of thing. How are we managing there?'

Fleming brightened but then seemed strangely hesitant. 'Ah…I had a stroke of luck there, sir. I managed to find a couple of impounded Norwegian tankers in New York and…' He hesitated and then rushed over the precipice. 'Well sir, Universal Exports now has a tanker fleet; only hired, not bought. And the ships are newly registered in Panama. The crews are Norwegian as well. The whole deal has cost a pretty packet and there's bound to be a hell of a row with the Norwegians but it really was the best I could do.'

The Major looked moodily at the tea. The whole Norwegian merchant fleet had been claimed by an exiled government who now sat not in Oslo but in London. The three-way war between the ship owners, Westminster and an emigre government struggling to find its place in a world where guns and expediency ruled, had only just been settled, though to no one's satisfaction and Fleming's action threatened that delicate balance.

Fleming had been watching the interplay between the man's face and the teacup.

'I really had no choice, sir,' he said with a trace of nervousness in his voice. 'Every other tanker is in full use.'

A brief vision of consigning every politician and ship owner to hell passed through the Major's mind and was instantly rejected as being of little help but Fleming had done well and needed to be told.

'No, I think you made the right call, Fleming. Our orders were to ensure the supply to Asturias and that's what you've done. The rest is politics. Men far higher up the pay grade than us will have to smooth those waters. I assume that both tankers are full?'

'Oh yes sir, almost full. Every kind of spirit and oil. Enough to last a while if the Asturians are careful.'

Fleming had done well, plucking two tankers from a well of ships that had run very dry indeed but there were bound to be repercussions. He foresaw battles and angry words ahead.

He dismissed his agent with kind words which were all the kinder for being heartfelt. He had been instructed to aid the Asturians without leaving any obvious signs that could be traced back to Washington or London, and Fleming had done just that. He took a sip of his insipid and cooling tea, hoping that its deceitful taste would improve with age. He forced himself to swallow it rather than waste a precious commodity. It was everyone's duty to avoid waste, just as it was his special duty to make things as difficult as he could for the Germans. And by giving the Asturians the results of spending donated American money, he hoped he had done just that.

Now the Asturians would see that they were not alone.

Now they could resist the unsubtle threats that had eddied and swirled their way via Lisbon that the routes north should be opened up once more.

Now they could hate once more.

Now it was up to them.

And Hitler.

The man's breath on his face was not pleasant but Oberst Kurt Steiner had faced far sterner challenges than an odour of half-digested vegetables. After all, facing those challenges was why he was here in Berlin in the first place.

He kept a grave expression on his face and stood stock still as the Führer placed the red and silver ribbon around his neck. He allowed

78

himself a very brief smile in response to Hitler's effusive words and responded with what he hoped was appropriate modesty. He saluted with parade ground precision and stood to one side as Hauptmann Ritter von Neustadt received a lesser, though much more decorative, medal.

The Neustadts had served the kings of Bavaria for five hundred years and Steiner knew exactly what his friend thought about the man who was even now receiving his stiff-armed salute.

There was no mockery in that salute of course. To do so here would be foolish and Neustadt was no fool. Besides he could see the Reichsmarschall staring at both of them from across the room.

The ceremony ended and the group of newly decorated men began to drift apart and make their way out into the labyrinth of corridors that led to lunch and, Steiner hoped, a welcome drink.

He saw Goering talk for a few moments with the Führer and gesture in their direction. Hitler nodded curtly and then vanished through the overly decorated doors.

'Parvenu.' Neustadt's voice was directed at the retreating Führer and was soft enough that only Steiner could hear it. He smiled at the word and kept the smile on his face as Goering walked swiftly over to them, arms stretched wide in welcome.

'Congratulations gentleman. You have much to smile about. To receive medals is a soldier's pleasure and his duty.' Goering's hand made an unconscious motion and touched the gold and blue enamelled medal that hung around his own neck. 'A fine lunch awaits us all gentleman but alas I must impose upon you for a few moments of your time.'

Steiner realised that the request was of course an order and he had little choice in the matter so they followed the blue uniformed body of his leader into a surprisingly sparse room covered in maps and photographs. He felt Neustadt tense behind him. Today was supposed to be a day of celebration, followed by a night spent in the less polite parts of Berlin but it was now obvious that those plans were at the very least postponed for now.

The Reichsmarschall was still smiling as he stood before them. 'As of this moment gentlemen, you are temporary members my staff. Your task is to plan and then lead an attack by Fallschirmjäger here.' He pointed to the map pinned to a large blackboard.

Steiner was careful not to let the surprise show on his face. There had been rumours, this was after all Berlin, the home of rumours. To see it as a potential reality was a shock.

'Operation Sonne,' the Luftwaffe contribution to the invasion of Northern Spain, which will be known as *Paladin* and involves all branches of the armed forces of the Reich but you gentlemen have been chosen to strike the first blow.'

Steiner did his best to look suitably honoured, while trying to grasp exactly how much danger he was going to inflict upon his men.

Goering's smile was now, the great beaming smile of one who has conferred a singular gift upon lesser beings. 'Your task is simple. All you have to do is to drop your men, seize the objective and hold until relieved. Offices have been arranged for you, and the Führer expects a detailed plan on his desk in two weeks.'

The smile dropped from Goering's face and Steiner saw the naked face of the Reichsführer. 'And so do I gentleman,' he continued. 'It's a simple operation and two weeks is more than enough time. A few weeks in Spain for you and then the Führer and I have other plans for you.'

Goering walked over to the table and a champagne bottle was opened with a muted pop and three glasses filled from it. 'Here's to your inevitable success and to Operation Sonne.' Goering's expansive smile was back but Steiner had seen the real man and knew that he and Neustadt had two weeks of intense work in front of them. He noticed that the bottle had been hastily stamped with the words Réservé à la Luftwaffe and hoped that was a good omen.

Goering left them with instructions to study the plans and then return to the lunch, telling them that copies of everything they would need would be delivered to their new offices.

Neustadt flicked idly through the folders and looked gloomily at the map. 'No night life for us, Herr Oberst.'

Steiner smiled warmly at his friend. 'Oh, but you are wrong Hans; very, very wrong. There will be plenty of night life, but spent arse deep in these folders.'

Neustadt face registered distaste and Steiner laughed at the man's discomfort. 'Come my friend it is not as bad as all that. After all we have access to Goering's champagne.

Neustadt's expression only deepened. 'Have you tasted it, Herr Oberst? The French have not sent their best.'

A second deeper sip confirmed Neustadt's first impression. The French army might have surrendered but the champagne growers had decided to continue the fight.

Steiner sighed, the day had taken a strange turn. He looked at the map, saw their own very special objective and his mind went back to childhood tales of knight errantry, of chivalrous deeds and honourable battle. Such things belonged to the past. Knight errantry was long dead but the land remained. Their objective was nothing but a mere line on the map, a rock-strewn cut where the bones of the earth showed through. Men and their causes had for centuries flowed back and forth along its length and uncounted drops of blood had aided its sparse fertility. Now another page had turned, blank as yet but soon to be filled with the red wounds of war.

The gates of Roncesvalles were about to be forced.

'La casa de mi madre tiene muchas puertas, pero pocas ventanas.'

The words dragged themselves up from the vaults of Dodd's memory as the inflatable boat pushed its way through the black water. Behind him was a half-submerged submarine, in front of him the coast of Spain, dimly illuminated by ghostly white breakers and weak starlight.

'The house of my mother has many doors but few windows.' Those were the first words in Spanish that he had truly understood. His teacher had been a kindly professor of comparative languages plucked from the comfort of a provincial university and sent to the bleak and wind ridden highlands of Scotland where Dodd and many others were being trained in the dark arts of sabotage and subversion.

They were the easy lessons, lessons that delighted but there were other lessons, harsher lessons under harder teachers. He learnt the many, many ways to kill, the staccato song of the Morse key flowing from his fingers, and the arts of spy-craft. All were revealed to him.

All these skills and more were carried within him towards the black painted land.

There was a sharp hiss from the leading seaman as a brief flash of light came from the shore and was repeated twice more.

'That's the signal sir,' said the sailor rather unnecessarily.

Dodd made no reply and the voice of the surf grew louder in his ears until a playful wave lifted the dinghy onto a pebble strewn beach. It took only a moment to deposit Dodd onto the damp beach and a further moment to thrust his baggage beside him, and then he was alone with only solid darkness for company.

He wasn't alone for long. A voice came out of the darkness and solid shapes emerged from the night revealing themselves into two familiar figures.

'Sargent Massu! Private Kanski!'

'The very same,' answered the thickset man with a short laugh. 'Are we not experts in finding lost Englishmen?'

'Who else would you expect to find on a lonely beach at this hour?'

Massu's French accented Spanish would have caused Dodd's old teacher to wince in agony but to Dodd's ears it was more than welcome. He grinned and shook hands with his old friends. Massu picked up the heavy radio with barely a grunt and they left the beach behind them.

Dodd was expecting a car or at the very least a truck. What he got was a mule and a surprise.

'The mule is not for you my friend,' Massu explained. 'Your radio does not have legs and you do - petrol is scarce and you are used to walking.'

Dodd grinned and began the long loping stride that was the hallmark of his regiment. He wondered what they would say if they knew that two tankers full of fuel were on their way to Gijón. That news alas he could not share but soon it would be common knowledge and he hoped his friends would forgive him.

His mission to the Asturians had begun.

THE DOLLS

'Still bearing 159 degrees, speed now around two hundred and fifty, height six thousand and descending.'

The radar's voice was a triumphant crackle.

They should be here soon, in fact right…about…now.'

Two barrel-chested aircraft screamed overhead and then turned, sharply climbing up through the low clouds and disappearing into their soft greyness.

A second pass received a stuttering light show from the Aldis Lamp and the aircraft departed, waggling their wings in farewell.

The Hood smiled. The Americans were peacetime warriors but were sharpening up nicely.

Somewhere over the horizon, far beyond even the radar's reach, lay a convoy escorted by American ships that dared the world to provoke them. But soon the convoy would be alone. American might would only stretch so far and the Hood and her sisters would take command from the moment the Americans reversed their course.

The Foxhound and her smaller sisters leapt away from the bigger ships and were soon lost amongst tall, white-capped waves.

She heard the destroyers and the corvettes exchange courtly greetings with the star-spangled ships whose voices faded as they turned from mock war to real peace.

It was time for the Hood to introduce herself. 'Welcome to my convoy. With luck you will never see me or any of my larger sisters but we will be close at hand though, so do not fear. My smaller sisters will be all around you. Obey their orders, stay in position and we will do our best to get you home. Now perhaps it would be as well if I got to know you.'

The first voice had echoes of ice and Arctic light. 'S. S Torvald here. My sister is the Bergen and we carry petrol and oils to Gijón.'

'Arundel Castle here, general cargo and the sooner I see the lights of Bristol the happier I'll be!'

'Alcoa Star, four days out, and full of the finest aluminium money can buy!'

'Empire Star, on my way to Gijón with these two crazy Norwegians. I'm carrying a load of tractors while my deck cargo is two of the strangest craft I've ever carried. They tell me that they are fishing boats but there must be mighty strange fish in Spain. That's all I can say!'

And so it went on. Forty-two ships introduced themselves, their accents coming from all around a war-wracked globe.

But there was still one voice missing, a voice the Foxhound had described. It was a hesitant voice, a voice beaten by time and ill-use. 'City of Chester...I'm the bundles for Bilbao ship.'

'And mighty pretty she looks.'

The giggling voice was full of scorn. The Hood was unable to place it but there was a low growl and a vision of sharp canines from the Foxhound and the giggling stopped abruptly. 'Please carry on,' she said, with pointed courtesy.

'I'm carrying medical supplies, canned food, dried milk, second hand clothes...and used dolls...lots of dolls and children's toys.'

The ships voice was miserable. This was obviously the end of a long spiralling career. 'I'm going to Gijón too,' the ship continued, 'if these guys don't mind.'

'I'm sure they won't.' She put a little iron in her voice and the two Norwegians took the hint and extended a welcome.

The Foxhound had described the old ship, covered in bunting and with two great American flags hastily painted over her seeping sides. It was not an attractive picture and the Hood understood the embarrassment. A little ripple of compassion ran through her so she decided to act in a way that all could hear. 'You have a cargo to be proud of. I am built for war; all my sisters are built for war. Within us you will find shells and bullets, explosives and mines. Whoever receives our cargo receives it not with joy but with fear. But you, you are different. Your cargo will feed the hungry and warm those that feel the winter chill. The sick will bless you, and children's eyes will shine once more when hawser ropes tie you to the shore. Truly you are on an honourable voyage.'

'Truly?'

'Truly. So much so that you will have the duty of leading the port column. Yours will be the honour of leading us home.'

She could almost see the little ship glow and across the far miles she heard that pride. 'Thank you, thank you so much.'

'You are welcome. Now if you will take your station, we may begin.'

It was a little bright moment in a warlike day and even the fifteen-inch mouths of her guns gave out gruff little coughs of approval. She now had a happy little steamer that felt better about herself and led, with bunting flying gaily, twenty bigger ships. No need to tell her that as the slowest ship, she alone determined the speed of the convoy. No need to tell her that if trouble struck her and she slowed further they would not wait for her and would pass her with only a brief farewell.

Better by far to let her keep her new-found pride and leave her with dignity intact.

And so the voyage began as so many had begun in peaceful and calm skies, the convoy and its escorts leading the way, with the Hood and her group trailing, ready to pounce if need compelled.

They sailed through dark Atlantic days and dark Atlantic nights until they reached the sullen no-man's land where skill pitted itself against skill in a game where losing was final and absolute, and luck was summoned by talismans that were worshipped with fervent belief.

It began as it always began with the four-engined bird that hung immutable and invulnerable over the convoy.

And then the nights became filled with blood.

The Arundel Castle would never see Bristol's docks again. The Alcoa Star dropped out, an invasive sea seeking out further holes in her scorched side. Ship after ship, night after night, died or was left behind.

And still the old ship pushed her rusting bows towards the east. She was scared, death was all around her but no word of fear did she utter. The place of honour was hers and she would not give way.

They were nearly home, a cursed moon standing high in the sky when the Hood heard a soft, drawn out wail and a last regretful word of sorrow and then there was nothing but a long howl of anger from the Foxhound.

She heard the hunt, heard the echoes of the depth charges, followed the battle as best she could, heard the Foxhound's bay of triumph and the corvette's satisfied 'That fixed the bastard.'

She sent her congratulations but nothing would bring back the old ship and her shining pride. Her blankets were gone and her medicines would now heal only fish but later that day as the Hood sailed over the wreck there was a sign that the ship had once lived. A horrid, macabre sign.

Dolls.

The sea was full of dolls.

Dolls of every description, some large, some small, some intact, others missing limbs. The waves gave them a dreadful mockery of life, and dead eyes and mirthless grins stared at her in mute accusation.

It was a graveyard she sailed over and she was very glad to leave but as she left, she offered up a last prayer for a gallant ship.

It had snowed that late November.

Snow was a rare event in Alabama, and this was only the second time in her short life that the white crystals had graced Maycomb with their presence. They turned out to be a fickle friends though, being only the heralds of a grey, persistent rain that hung around like an unwelcome relative.

Jean Louise Finch, known to the world as 'Scout' was trapped, imprisoned by a damp jailer. Games and even her books had long since lost their appeal. She roamed the house listening to the drip and hiss of the downpour. In desperation she entered her father's study.

Atticus was listening to the radio, head cocked to one side, and glasses perched precariously on his head.

She sat silently, not wishing to break his concentration.

The radio issued a last farewell and the glasses were replaced so that her father could see her. She complained of boredom, of having boundless energy with no outlet. There was silence for a moment while her father realised that the old Jean Louise was changing before his eyes, the uncomplicated child being chipped away day by day.

What lay beneath only time could tell but he still had the opportunity to do a little subtle carving. 'It seems to me, Scout,' he said slowly, 'as if you need to count your blessings. Seems to me that you need a little perspective. Maybe see that a little rain isn't such a big problem. Maybe you should look out through someone else's eyes and see what the world looks like to them.'

He reached out and grasped a book and pushed it into her reluctant hands. 'Read this. Then come back and tell me how big your problems really are. Now go and wash your hands; supper is nearly ready.'

She followed the smell of food, discarding the book in favour of building a growing body but later despairing of ever seeing the outdoors again she began to read.

The book had a photograph of a small child protectively clutching a doll on its dust cover and the title 'No Need For Fame' in plain black letters. Like every child of her age Scout looked at the photographs. The pictures showed a people under great strain. They showed bloodied doctors operating with desperate skill, thin children being taught by haggard teachers in damp cellars. They showed grimly smiling mothers making meals out of less than nothing, and finally they showed a tall muscular man wrapped in a greasy sheepskin coat laughing at the camera.

The rain clouds still lowered over Maycomb, and she began to read.

'Atticus this just ain't fair.' She held the book in her hand and faced her father.

'Isn't fair, Scout,' Atticus corrected his angry daughter. 'What isn't fair?'

The book was waved like a battle flag in Scout's hand. 'This ain't...isn't fair. There's these people way over in Spain and they are getting shot and bombed and such, and it isn't fair'

Atticus gazed on his red faced daughter, who had forgotten about the rain in her anger.

'There's children Atticus without school books, and doctors that ain't got no medicine and...and...' She slowed, the anger she felt fighting with the words in her head.

A small glow of pride warmed her father. His daughter may be growing but the essential goodness in her and her fierce sense of justice remained and would remain. He was sure of that now.

'Why are they doing this Atticus? Why is that Franco bombing them and fightin' them?'

'Because the Asturians said "No," Scout. It's as simple as that.'

Scout's outrage grew even greater. 'No. All those people in the book just plain suffering, because of a word?'

'It's not the word, Scout, it's the intent behind the word. The Asturians and a few other people decided that they didn't want to be ruled by General Franco, so they said *No*.' Sometimes the simplest words are the most powerful.'

'Atticus it says in the book that they have a Declaration of Independence like ours.'

'It amounts to the same thing, Scout. All declarations of independence are peoples saying the same word. As long as they keep saying that word they will continue to suffer.'

'The book says we should help. Right at the end Atticus, it says we should help.'

It was then that Atticus laid his trap. 'And?'

Sometimes the simplest words are the most powerful.

She hated the dress, and the pearl necklace she treated with indifference but today she wore both and stood gravely in what she fervently hoped was a genteel manner, handing out sweet cake to the women of the Ladies Missionary society.

She summoned up every last particle of courage and addressed what she believed was the most sympathetic person in the room.

'Miss Atkinson I've been reading Miss Gellhorn's book.'

There was an expression of distaste from Stephanie Crawford and a swift exchange of glances between Atkinson and her Aunt Alexandria.

'Really Jean Louise? Isn't that a little heavy for you? Well perhaps not. Have you read it Stephanie? It really is an excellent book.'

Scout caught a fading glimmer of humour in her aunt's eyes and realised that somehow Maude Atkinson was teasing the thin-lipped woman.

The reply was just as thin as the lips that issued it. 'I most certainly have not!'

Atkinson's returning smile seemed genuine. 'Such a shame Stephanie. It would amply repay you; perhaps you could borrow my copy.'

She turned back to Scout the mysterious interchange now over. 'You were saying dear?'

'Well I was thinking that maybe I could help like it says in the book. Me and Jem could organise a play and charge people money to see it. We could go around doing the play on people's lawns - we could put adverts in the paper. Dill writes poetry. He could read out poems and such. I bet people would pay ten cents to hear one of Dill's poems. He wrote a poem about me once and it was real good, and...'

She stopped, suddenly aware that the entire room was staring at her.

'I just want to help.' Her words seemed very small in the room but as she had hoped she got a sympathetic response from Miss Atkinson.

'And it shows, child. It is a truly Christian response.' Atkinson looked around the room. 'Well isn't it?'

The challenge was laid down and to Scout's surprise her aunt picked up the gauntlet. 'Of course, it is Maude, and from what I hear the Asturians are quite fashionable in Washington right now.'

'Yankees!'

The single word was full of scorn but her Aunt's smile remained bright. 'Not so Stephanie. Why I was reading only last week about the Governor's wife and how she's organising a fund drive to raise money for those poor people.' Aunt Alexandria's voice was only gently chiding. She was a Southern lady born and raised, and never, ever forgot her manners. But she was in charge and Scout realised, that without planning it, she had gained an ally.

'Now the question is whether Maycomb can hold its head up if it refuses to follow where the Governor's wife has pointed.' Her eyes tracked around the room. 'I for one refuse to believe that an upstanding, God-fearing community such as we have here will not do its utmost to help when called upon, and it is only a pity that it took a child to point out the way.'

Scout was the puzzled but grateful recipient of a rare beaming smile from her aunt.

Atticus had, in an unguarded moment, called his sister "A force of nature,' and even he picked his battles with her only after much thought. The men of Maycomb recognised the inevitable and fell like young saplings in a high wind.

The Baptists played the Methodists in a game of touch football and raised twenty seven dollars and seventy five cents.

Every house had at least two overpriced pound cakes waiting to be eaten and there were more pot luck suppers in one month than in the previous twelve, each and every one of them raising more money.

Jem and Scout did indeed perform their play and Dill's poems were received by men who sat with gritted teeth, their pockets lighter by ten cents.

By Christmas time all was ready and Scout stood on the railway platform while her only doll and many others were loaded on the rail car. A check for over a hundred and seventy dollars was already winging its way north and would be a small addition to a growing sum.

The Reverend Sykes gave a signal and Zebo led the choir in a rousing rendition of *Oh what a friend we have in Jesus*.

It was, Aunt Alexandria declared, a triumph, tasteful without being too extreme, and the hand-written letter she received from the Governor's mansion became a treasured possession.

Christmas came and went as did the rain and Scout followed the journey of her doll through articles in the newspapers which were pasted with care in her scrapbook.

The newest page showed the City of Chester leaving port and joining other ships bound for Europe.

Then came other news, unwelcome, heart-breaking news.

Her father had stood in her doorway grim faced, evening paper in hand. Her ship had been sunk. There was a grainy photograph taken from a British warship that showed the sea covered in broken dolls. She searched in vain for her own doll but could not see it.

The photograph joined the others but this one was stained with tears.

Time passed. Bob Hope and Jack Benny made pointed jokes about Nazi doll-killers and there was a tense exchange of notes between Washington and Berlin but her doll was still lost and there could never be another round of baking while Maycomb was undoubtedly sick of pot luck suppers.

She brooded for a while, thinking of her doll lost and afraid on the ocean instead of comforting a child far away, and then she did the only thing she could think of doing.

She wrote to the President.

It was early March now, winter had lost its sting and spring's faint voice was beginning to be heard. Atticus was dressed and breakfasted and was already half way out of the door when the telephone rang.

Scout was only half listening.

'Eula May, if this is some kind of joke, I'll have Heck Tate arrest you so fast your head will spin. Very well I'll take the call but heaven help you if...Yes speaking.

'Yes, sir. I was aware that she had...

'No sir, I didn't help at all. Those are her words not mine...

'Really, he is?

'Yes sir, I will...

'No sir, not a word...

'Thank you, sir. Goodbye.'

Atticus put down his hat and returned to the kitchen. He stood for a moment looking at his daughter with absolute amazement and then vanished once more.

They had gathered around the radio waiting for the valves to warm up enough to gather the invisible voices from the air. Then the familiar voice of Franklin Roosevelt broke through the speakers.

'My fellow Americans. Some time ago I received a letter from a little girl in Maycomb, Alabama; a little girl named Jean Louise.'

Scout stiffened and her mouth opened in shock at hearing her name, she was about to speak but Atticus placed a gentle finger over her mouth as Roosevelt continued to speak.

'Like many of you she contributed to the aid that was sent to the peoples of Northern Spain; aid freely given by a free people to men, women and children who were suffering from want of the basic necessities of life. Sadly, as you all know, the ship carrying that aid was sunk and Jean Louise asks, and rightly asks, what is to be done and in particular what I as president will do?

'Before I get to that, I would like to make it very clear that the City of Chester was clearly marked as an American ship and was sailing with non-contraband goods. There can be no question about that just as there can be no question that the submarine was of Nazi origin. The leaders of Germany have admitted that this is the case but no apology, no admission of mistake, no offer of reparations has come from their Government. The United States ship, when attacked, was proceeding on a legitimate peaceful voyage.

'The position of the United States government is plain. If the City of Chester was visible to the submarine when the torpedo was fired, then the attack was a deliberate attempt by the Nazis to sink a clearly identified American ship. On the other hand, if the submarine was beneath the surface of the sea and, with the aid of its listening devices, fired in the direction of the sound of the American ship without even taking the trouble to learn its identity, as the official German communique would indicate, then the attack was even more outrageous. For it indicates a policy of indiscriminate violence against any vessel sailing the seas, belligerent or non-belligerent.

'This is piracy, piracy legally and morally.

'It was not the first nor the last act of piracy which the Nazi Government has committed against ships bearing the American flag, for attack has followed attack. In light of this act of Nazi aggression, we as Americans must take a long-range point of view in regard to certain fundamentals of self-defence, for most assuredly the sinking of a peaceful merchantman is evidence which makes it clear that the incident is not isolated but part of a general plan, and it would be folly to pretend otherwise.

'The important truth is that these acts of international lawlessness are a manifestation of a design which has been made clear to the

American people for a long time. It is the Nazi design to abolish the freedom of the seas, and to acquire absolute control and domination of these seas for themselves.

'For with control of the seas in their own hands, the way can be cleared for their next step. Domination of the United States, domination of the Western Hemisphere by force of arms.

'Under Nazi control of the seas, no merchant ship of the United States would be free to carry on any peaceful commerce, except by the condescending grace of this foreign and tyrannical power.

'The Atlantic Ocean which has been, and which should always be, a free and friendly highway for us would then become a deadly menace to the commerce of the United States, to the coasts of the United States, and even to the inland cities of the United States.

'The Hitler Government, in defiance of the laws of the sea, in defiance of the recognized rights of all other Nations, has presumed to declare, on paper, that great areas of the seas, including a vast expanse lying in the Western Hemisphere are to be closed, and that no ships may enter them for any purpose, except at peril of being sunk.

'In brief we must take the sinking of the City of Chester as a warning to the United States not to resist the Nazi movement of world conquest. It is a warning that the United States may use the high seas of the world only with the consent of the Nazis. Were we to yield on this point we would eventually be forced to yield on others and that is a path that leads to Nazi domination and the ultimate extinction of America and the ideals for which she stands.

'We are not yielding and do not propose to yield. No act of violence, no act of intimidation will keep us from maintaining intact two bulwarks of American defence. First, our line of supply of materiel to the enemies of Hitler; and second, the freedom of our shipping on the high seas. No matter what it takes, no matter what it costs, we will keep open the lines of legitimate commerce.

'We have sought no shooting war with Hitler. We do not seek it now but neither do we want peace so much that we are willing to pay for it by permitting him to attack our merchant ships while they are on legitimate business.

'I assume that the German leaders are not deeply concerned, tonight or any other time, by what we Americans or the American Government say or publish about them. We cannot bring about the downfall of Nazism by the use of long-range invective. But when you see a rattlesnake poised to strike, you do not wait until he has struck before you crush him. These Nazi submarines and raiders are the rattlesnakes of the Atlantic. They are a menace to the free pathways of the high seas. They are a challenge to our sovereignty. They hammer at our most precious rights when they attack ships of the American flag—symbols of our independence, our freedom, our very life.

'It is clear to all Americans that the time has come when America itself must now be defended, for if submarines or raiders attack in distant waters, they can attack equally well within sight of our own shores.

'So, to Jean Louise I say that the time for active defence is now...this Jean Louise is the time for prevention of attack.

'In the waters which we now deem necessary for our defence, American naval vessels and American planes will no longer wait until Axis submarines lurking under the water, or Axis raiders on the surface of the sea, strike their deadly blows.

Upon our naval and air patrol, now operating in large number over a vast expanse of the Atlantic Ocean falls the duty of maintaining the American policy of freedom of the seas. That means, very simply, very clearly, that our patrolling vessels and planes will protect all merchant ships, not only American ships but ships of any flag engaged in commerce in our defensive waters. They will protect them from submarines, they will protect them from surface raiders. The attack on the City of Chester is a clarion call to all of us and as President my obligation is historic, it is clear, it is inescapable.

'It is no act of war on our part when we decide to protect the seas that are vital to American defence. The aggression is not ours. We act only out of defence, out of protecting what we and our forebears have painfully built. But let this warning be clear. From now on, if German or Italian vessels of war enter the waters, the protection of which is necessary for American defence, they do so at their own peril.

'The orders which I have given as Commander in Chief of the United States Army and Navy are to carry out that policy at once and without hesitation.

'The sole responsibility rests upon Germany. There will be no shooting unless Germany continues to seek it.

'This is our clear right as a sovereign Nation. It is the only step possible, if we wish to save our children and our children's children from terrorism and slavery. I have no illusions about the gravity of this step. I have not taken it hurriedly or lightly. It is the result of months and months of constant thought and anxiety and prayer but in the protection of your Nation and mine, it cannot be avoided.

'The American people have faced other grave crises in their history, with American courage, and with American resolution, they will do no less today.

'They know the actualities of the attacks upon us, they know the necessities of a bold defence against these attacks. They know that the times call for clear heads and fearless hearts. And with the inner strength that comes to a free people conscious of their duty, and conscious of the righteousness of what they do, they will...with Divine help and guidance stand their ground against this assault upon their democracy, their sovereignty, and their freedom.'

Atticus turned the radio off and looked at his children. Jem was looking a little shocked. The President had mentioned his sister. But Scout had unadulterated fear in her eyes, which filled with tears. 'I did it, it's my fault.' The emerging adult had vanished and it was the small child that threw herself into her father's arms, terrified that her letter might have plunged the United States into war.

It took all of Atticus's considerable courtroom skill and every ounce of his humanity to convince Scout that America's foreign policy was not decided upon a single letter, no matter how heartfelt or how well written.

He tried to explain the long tortuous process that must have preceded the President's decision. He explained as best he could the behind the scenes promises that would be kept or broken, the late-night phone calls, the meetings that went on until dawn's light broke through traffic stained windows.

'So, you see Scout your letter was used by the President to show people that even a small child could see that this country is in danger. Why I believe that the President had probably made up his mind before your letter even arrived.'

The tears stopped and the shuddering breaths slowed. The eyes which had showed terror and then tears now began to droop with fatigue. Nature was taking refuge from emotional storms in that most secure of bastions, the isle of sleep.

Atticus picked up his daughter and placed her in her bed where she dreamt. She dreamt of brave ships that lived and died with pride, of dolls that missed their destiny and a land far away where people spoke powerful, simple words. Words that had been said many times and were soon to be repeated before a force that did not accept denial.

PALADIN

Outside was Death.

Cold.

Airless.

Watching.

A moments mistake, a tiny error and Death would seize him and drag his feeble body into his black kingdom.

But not today. Today he was a king with his own kingdom spread out brown and green below him. Above him were the clouds, pink with the light of a new born sun. Inside their folds lay safety where he could hide, immune from the enemy.

But not today. Today his task was to seek and not to hide. Sparkling sun glinted on needle-thin rivers, hamlets a thousand years in the ground passed beneath him. On and on he flew. Engine strongly beating. Wings gently lifting. Until he was sure that this was the time, that this was the place.

He pointed the nose down, half hearing the engine roar, then levelled out and flew across his kingdom.

Flew while the great glassy eyes sought out every secret.

Flew while marching men, horses, and trucks were caught forever on film.

Flew while serried rows of aircraft were laid naked before the camera's flickering shutter.

Then, his work done, he climbed. Climbed, twisting towards heaven. Climbed, while angry shrapnel broke in impotent fiery breaths.

Run now.

Run. Leaving a kingdom far behind.

Run. While fuel and life remain.

Run for home.

Paladin.

He had caught *Paladin.*

Worry was a constant companion, and he doubted that any Prime Minister had a companion who peered so grimly over his shoulder. He opened the folder once more, hoping that there would be a way to dismiss his companion, even for a while.

There was not.

The photographs were damning. The airfields, full of men and equipment, the labouring locomotives pulling the battle proven tanks through a war-weary France, all had been discovered. More damning yet were the messages pulled from the air and teased and tortured by subtle and clever men to reveal their secrets.

He could not tell the Asturians that great machines whirled and hummed through many nights to break the unbreakable.

Paladin, the messages whispered. The name was mentioned by men of high rank and of low.

He knew or at least half-knew the secrets that the Germans held.

But he could not tell them. To reveal even a little now would be to reveal all and that he could not do. He could not tell the Asturians that an armoured fist was about to hammer on their door, that their healing land must suffer once again. This was the agony that he must suffer, that brave men must die, though a mere word from him could save so many of them.

The Nazis must never suspect that an obscure country house had prised open their coding machines and revealed a great treasure. Many men had died in defence of that knowledge and the Asturians were now to join that long list.

He could not tell them but though they must take the first blows, they would not suffer alone.

He took a reflective sip of brandy, which did a little to soothe his spirits. It seemed that the next few days were going to be busy. The Germans were about to stick their neck out. It only remained to be seen how sharp his blade was.

Night.

The night was black.

Soft.

Yielding.

Birds. The sky was full of great metal birds. Row after row, layer after layer. Their engines rent the black sky and their fashioned wings cleaved the air.

Men. The sky was full of men swaying in the air. Line after line, silken sheet after silken sheet of men drifting towards the receiving earth.

Below them was Roncesvalles.

And war.

The ground reached out and punched Hans in the legs, transmitting the shock through his spine and into his head. His eyes shook for a dangerous few seconds.

The blackness was absolute. He stretched out a hand before him and it vanished as if transported to another realm. Only sound could aid him now. He heard a gasp and a familiar ripping sound as a parachute gracefully collapsed. Now he heard a familiar voice gently swearing as the once graceful parachute began to fill out once more with the night air.

'Otto is that you?'

He was rewarded by the sound of Feldwebel Brant and together they began the task of gathering men and equipment. At last their leader joined them and Steiner led them up the pass.

The war in Spain had begun.

It was a typical Spanish crucifix, grisly and more than a little macabre. It lay amongst the rubble untouched with only a fine patina of dust coating the gilded surface. He reached down, amazed that amongst all the death, amongst all the irreversible destruction, this tiny piece of artwork had survived. His fingers wiped away the dust and an agonised Christ stared accusingly back at him.

It had all gone so well, they had entered the town unnoticed and unannounced.

In less than an hour the town was theirs. The town garrison was either killed or had fallen back in disturbingly good order, and the road to the landing strip beckoned invitingly. But along that road, lying like a rock between the town and the landing strip, lay the convent.

For a thousand years weary travellers, and eager pilgrims had dragged their bodies through its gates and found cooling water, a rough meal and kind words to speed them on their way.

The building had been made for the glory of God and much care had been lavished on it. Its finely cut stones had defied centuries that had brought heat and cold, howling snows and blazing suns. Its great beams were an oaken team that regarded the years with indifference, and such was the skill of their builders that a load felt by one was a load felt by all.

But now bullets had taken the place of breviaries, and soft words by harsh curses. The convent now had troops whose guns covered the landing strip and its walls laughed at the puny weapons of Steiner's men.

Hauptmann Ritter von Neustadt was by his side as they gazed at the defiant walls. 'They won't surrender Herr Oberst.'

'Would you Hans? They are brave men with a duty to perform.'

Steiner beckoned a heavily built corporal who carried the radio set with ease and spoke the word that he had always known must be spoken.

The Stuka pilots were veterans of Poland and France. Their aim was well practised and true. The stones were blasted and the beams were sundered, flames consuming in seconds tapestries that were the work of generations. The Fallschirmjäger moved through the broken walls killing the dazed survivors. The convent was theirs and Steiner was left holding the strangely untouched image of Christ.

A tiny shiver passed through him. It was not shame; a soldier should feel no shame; he done no more than his duty, but it was certainly regret. The agonised face continued to stare at Steiner until he gently placed the cross back amongst the rubble turned away.

The garrison had fought to the last but there was still much to do before the airfield could be made ready for the aircraft which were already on their way. His men threw off the fatigue of battle and began the tasks which would allow the much-needed reinforcements to land.

The welcome sound of BMW engines was already in the air when a puzzled Feldwebel Brant reported to Steiner. 'Herr Oberst we found the wires to the explosives and traced them to the landing strip but when we dug down, we found only rocks and this.' He held out a glass jar which held a sheet of paper.

The jar was opened and Steiner read the hastily scrawled message,

Muerte de los Alemanes!

'Only rocks, Sergeant. No explosives?'

'Just rocks, Herr Oberst.'

An icy hand gripped his heart and he turned to the radio operator. 'Contact the flight leader. Tell him to abort!'

It was too late.

The first two transports were already committed to landing and though they did not know it they were already dead. The first shell landed just in front of the lead aircraft, eviscerating it and all who sat inside. The second landed behind the following aircraft, the blast wave picking it up like a child's toy and smashing its burning remains back on to the grass.

Several more shells ensured that the airfield would be unusable for anything larger than birds for the foreseeable future and the German reinforcements turned for home or a fuel starved forced landing as the shells continued to fall.

Von Neustadt gazed wonderingly up the sheer-sided cliff face where thin wisps of smoke gave evidence of the cannon's position. 'They dragged a gun up that?'

'So it would seem, Hans. We were warned were we not? Our opponents are masters of surprise and subterfuge. Well, we were surprised.'

'What now, Herr Oberst?'

'We pray Hans. We pray that there are no more surprises in store for us, we pray that our relief column comes up the valley in time.'

They watched as two prowling fighters fired at the cliff face and then pulled up sharply before the rocks ate them.

The cannon fired one more time and then was silent.

Von Neustadt smiled.

'Well that is one prayer answered, Herr Oberst. As for the rest I will take my chances, and after all we're in a convent. Is there a better place to pray?'

Steiner did not answer. He stared first at the crucifix and then at the stark message on the paper.

The garrison had fought to the last man and the gun's crew must surely have known that theirs was a mission that could have only one ending. Yet all had sacrificed themselves without hesitation. 'Muerte de los Alemanes!' he mumbled.

'Herr Oberst?'

'Nothing Hans, nothing. We'll set up here. I want covering positions over there and see if you can salvage some of those heavy machine guns. I have a feeling they may come in useful.

Muerte de los Alemanes! Steiner thought. *How do you fight a people who would think such a thing and would die before surrendering?* He gazed down again at the crucifix. Was it his imagination or did the image of Christ now have a sardonic expression on its face? Whatever the expression, he was certain now of one thing.

This was not going to be a short war.

'It's not too late laddie. The vestry door is just there. Make a run now and I'll hold them off.'

Pulver had learnt many words in the Navy and although he knew the old engineer was joking, he decided to use a few of them to relieve the tension. Using the same soft voice, he grinned and turned to the old man. 'Why don't you just...'

At that moment the organist began an over enthusiastic rendition of the wedding march.

'Too late laddie, she's here.'

Pulver's sense of humour had vanished with the first few notes of the music. 'Do you have the ring?'

There was a smile and the old man patted a breast pocket. 'All present and correct laddie; no need to panic; she's a bonnie wee thing, treat her well.'

The vicar stepped forward and he could feel the grey-green eyes shining at him.

'Dearly beloved...'

The bride's dress was borrowed, the cake took the rations of both families and the hall was booked for just a few hours. This was a wartime wedding after all.

But some things never change; both mothers cried, the bridesmaids fought over the bouquet and both fathers danced like crippled penguins.

The old engineer made a speech which was both grave and funny and read out telegrams from those who could not attend. Except one, Pulver noticed. One that was read very carefully and then placed in his breast pocket. Was the old engineers smile a little forced after that? He couldn't tell and soon the incident was forgotten in the cloud of good wishes and doubtful advice that surrounded him.

It was later when the last of the guests were leaving that his best man cornered him. It was typical of the man that he was direct. 'Your leave's been cancelled, laddie.' He heard a gasp behind him and a delicate hand tighten on his own.

'I got the telegram with the others, I didn't read it of course.' He looked at the girl who now had tears in her eyes. 'I'm sorry lassie but it looks like that man has done it again.' He pulled out the evening paper and showed Pulver the glaring headlines announcing the invasion of Spain. 'Unless I miss my guess, you'll be going South. In any event your train leaves at seven tomorrow.'

He gave them a wintery smile. 'I've booked you a hotel for the night and your travel warrants will be waiting for you at the station. You've one night, Mr and Mrs Pulver. Make the best of it.'

The humorous mention of her new name brought a trembling, hesitant smile and she remembered her promise that come what may she would be worthy of her husband. She dashed away the tears and thanked the old man with words that brought out a new respect in him.

Her husband was going back to the war...her war. And she would be worthy of him.

Come what may.

The boilers voices were wheezy and asthmatic as could only be expected from beings that burnt gallons of thick oil every day.

'We are doing our best, perhaps enough steam for steerage way in twenty minutes. Are you sure you won't wait for the tugs?'

She knew the boilers were doing all they could but it was her duty to check. 'Quite sure.' she answered, 'my orders are specific "with all possible despatch" they say and we have a troop convoy to escort so there's no time to waste.'

Her children had caught the excitement and were whispering excitedly amongst themselves.

'We're going to play.'

'And shoot.'

'And have fun, so much fun.'

'We should leave now, why can't we leave now?'

She smiled. Her children could wait while she checked on the great turbines and whirling drive shafts that would speed her on her way.

At last the boilers agreed to release the captive steam and beneath her, tons of finely crafted bronze began to turn.

She was off to war.

'A little more to port please.' The Hood's voice was calm and soothing and they heard nothing of the strain she felt.

Grease wrapped screws turned, oiled pistons pushed and a groaning rudder heaved against the Bay of Biscay.

'Like that?'

'That's wonderful,' she said, 'now midships if you can.'

The rudder groaned again, not understanding why its simple life was now so busy but she knew. She knew why her boilers were swallowing gallons of oil. She knew why her bow crushed wave after wave with speedy might.

She knew why she was entering waters that had seen ponderous galleys and sharp beaked privateers, stately three decker's and prosperous merchantmen.

Men and guns.

Men and tanks.

Men and aircraft.

An army was on the move, an army of veterans and of those new to war.

An army bound for Spain.

'Here they come.' The Radar's warning was heard by her children who cheered and then giggled expectantly. 'Six aircraft coming down now.'

The battle had begun.

She and her sisters turned, leaving foaming curves in the sea. Red balls of fire flew from them in deadly sine waves.

A destroyer lurched as a bomb hit her and she felt the pain but the convoy moved on.

A bomber, already in flames was given a farewell burst from her Vickers machine guns.

She turned sharply, waves breaking over her bow in a flurry of salt scented rainbows and a bomb aimed for her heart burst in the uncaring sea.

An aircraft swooped down on her and her children gave out smoke-filled laughs and it vanished into streaming flames.

'Oh that was well done, which one of you did that?'

There was an excited gasp from one the starboard four-point-fives. 'I think that was me.'

'Well it was well done, whoever it was.'

They basked in the glow of her voice and sent more messages of death to the black painted aircraft.

A broken-backed troop ship sank and the sea was covered in oil and the heads of drowning men but the convoy moved on.

The enemy sent small, swift moving boats and she ordered the Foxhound and her smaller sisters forward and they swept down on them like wolves, turbines howling, guns barking. They burst out of the waves, killing, and turning and killing again in a well-practiced and deadly dance.

And the convoy moved on.

On and on until the fading sun illuminated the shores of Spain.

And a new war.

He watched the old woman run through the rubble of the town. Her black dress was torn and hid thin, arthritic legs but she still ran. Her toothless mouth uttered the words that had become so familiar over the past few weeks. "Muerte de los Alemanes!"

Her voice was thin and broken but the sound came clearly down the narrow street as she picked up a fallen rifle and dived head first into the remains of a shop that in happier times had sold linen.

Two ill aimed shots rang out and Steiner winced.

The woman should be tending her grandchildren, telling them tales of kings and queens, of magic slippers and trees than grew to the sky, not shooting at his men.

Another shot rang out and this time there was a curse from one of his men.

It was likely though that her grandchildren were dead, lost in the rubble, and certainly this was no tale to have a happy ending. This was their fourth week in Spain and the pattern was now all too familiar.

Three days he had held the convent and the town of Roncesvalles. Three days while the Fallschirmjäger fought for their lives. Three days and three nights while they died one by one.

It was a much smaller band that cheered the clattering, screeching tanks and the dust-coated troops that marched through the burning town and down the road to the ruined building that had become the first victim of this new war.

They had followed the tanks, followed the trail of smoke and of dead men, past the burnt out vehicles and fields scorched by bitter farmers.

And now they were here, days behind schedule and many kilometres from where they should be. This was not France, still less was this Holland; this was a land fuelled by bitter enmity where every man's hand was against them.

This was not war, or if it was, then it was a war not of swords that cut savagely but of Spanish knives that drew a little blood and then vanished only to return and cut again.

All their campaigns had been quick, over before the enemy could respond but this enemy slowly retreated and all the time harried the precious supplies that weaved their way through captured valleys along roads that were the despair of Quartermasters and Engineers alike.

Somewhere in front of them were the enemy armies, tormented by an overstretched Luftwaffe but still elusive, still waiting for their supply lines to stretch even tighter, for their fatigue to become even more numbing.

A stream of high-pitched insults came from the ruined shop, followed by a further, more accurate shot. Steiner sighed; the old woman must die, perhaps to join her grandchildren. He signalled to Feldwebel Brant and his men began to lay down covering fire while Brant moved forward with one of their precious grenades.

Amazingly the covering fire did not work and the old woman stood up, moving much faster than her age should allow and fired, hitting Brant in the chest. He fell, followed seconds later by the old woman who was almost cut in two by machine gun fire, her last defiant words still leaving her mouth.

It took hours to take the town, for the old woman had passed on her hate but as the sun set, they ate their scanty rations and drank gritty water in the ruins.

The road west was open.

And as the sentries nervously patrolled, as the sun sank back into the land, as Steiner fitfully slept, a new army arrived in Spain. The last redcoats had left over a hundred years ago and only legends remained of their battles but now their sons had returned.

To make new legends.

A thousand voices sang as one.

The song was both a challenge and a promise.

The song was their history and a goad to their enemies.

They formed up on the dockside, turned as one and then still singing marched off with a long loping stride that was designed to eat up the miles. It was a sight worth seeing. Jorge had wished for allies, even prayed to a god he did not believe in for allies, and now they were here. Not of course for his sake, nor for his new fledged country; he was realist enough to understand that. They were here for their own purposes and their own reasons. But they were here and that was the main thing.

He turned to Dodd who was looking with shining and longing eyes at the backs of the marching men. 'They are good soldiers, my friend?'

Dodd gave a wistful smile. 'They are the Rifles, General. They are my regiment, and yes they are very good soldiers.'

Jorge had come to know Dodd by now and knew the source of the smile. 'And you wish to join your regiment?'

The smile vanished. 'My place is with you, General.'

'So it is. Now let us go meet your British General. Let us see what kind of man he is.'

It was a long walk up to the end of the docks where a man in a battered battledress was supervising the unloading of trucks and scout cars. This seemed an odd task for a general but Dodd assured him that this was indeed the man the British had sent.

The man turned and smiled, and Jorge was shocked. The man was old! He wore thick horn-rimmed glasses and his hair had become grey and thin. Jorge had hoped for a young general, a fighting general but this was obviously a refugee from a desk. His heart sank though he was careful not to let it show.

The man spoke and Dodd translated. 'My name is Percy Hobart and I am pleased to meet you at last, I have heard much about you.' He took off his glasses and Jorge saw that perhaps he was mistaken, for there was a good deal of shrewdness that lay behind them.

'Together we will give the Germans a bloody nose and make him sorry he ever crossed the border.'

Jorge heard the translated words and smiled, he was a peasant and this was war, not a boxing match. Though he appreciated the sentiment, he wished to give the enemies of his country more than a nose bleed. He pointed to his groin and spoke to a grinning Dodd.

'Jorge says that he thinks we should do more, he thinks...' Dodd struggled for a moment, wondering whether he should give a direct translation of what had been said. At last discretion won out and he weakened Jorge's crude words. '...he thinks we should emasculate the Germans sir, every last one of them.'

To the surprise of both of them Hobart merely nodded his head in agreement and then laughed. 'Yes, and that is what we shall do...together.' The laughter vanished, and the glasses once more hid the intelligent eyes. Hobart straightened his battledress and pointed towards the now empty ship. 'Now, if my staff, have done as they were asked, I am ready for our first planning meeting. I am anxious to hear your thoughts on just how we emasculate our enemy.'

The Second Peninsula war had begun.

HOBSON'S CHOICE

Joachim Ribbentrop was a happy man.

He had made promises. Many promises. And threats.

The threats were lesser in number, for behind him lay an army and the threats were there for all to see. And perhaps the promises would be kept; perhaps the guns and the aircraft would be delivered; perhaps the oil and wheat would at least trickle over the border. Perhaps the Führer would restore the Asturian and the Basque lands to Spain. Perhaps Spain would expand its empire in Africa.

Or then again perhaps not.

Certainly, the Spanish people would suffer because of today but then they were suffering already and their agonies were no concern of his.

Certainly because of today his rise would be assured and his influence restored.

But today was the day a most reluctant Spain was forced into an alliance with Germany. Today was the day Spain joined the Axis powers.

He smiled. Soon the Basques and the Asturians would be defeated and their British allies would once more be forced back into the sea. His heart quickened at the thought.

After such a defeat surely even the British would sue for peace or at least an armistice and then the way would be open for a final reckoning with the Bolsheviks.

The scenes unfolded in his mind. A peace treaty signed by a trembling London, a burning Moscow with Stalin lying in its ashes and the German foreign office dictating treaties and pacts that would ensure Berlin's supremacy for generations. All this and much more was possible now. All this was his to direct and control.

With Spain safely within the Axis fold, Portugal would be sure to follow, and then the whole Atlantic coast and the Mediterranean would become a happy playground--where only a few would be allowed to play.

His smile broadened as an expressionless Spanish Foreign Minister signed the treaty. In his eyes, from that moment on Spain was a colony of the German Reich.

But if he had used his ears, he would have heard the barely formed scars of the civil war being ripped away.

Portugal. First. Last. Always.

If there was a single lode stone in Antonio Salazar's life it was this. Any other consideration, any other interest could not match this simple mantra. He saw his duty plainly, and if others saw events in a different light then they were wrong.

He had lived a life of intellect, free of doubt. Until now.

He could not hear the guns, he could not hear the snarling engines of the bombers. He could not see the swarming armies, the bodies or the burning. And yet they were real and they existed. Scant miles away they existed and grew closer and louder.

The Asturians had allies now but doubt remained. The cards were falling, twisting and turning as they fell from God's own hands into the laps of eager players. And now despite his wishes, despite his prayers he was a player, though a most reluctant one.

God had, in his wisdom placed so few cards in his hand. So very few. He had moved Portugal's army up to the border. His navy now leaked steam from every seldom used engine.

He had no illusions.

His army would be routed and his navy sunk, not in a month, nor yet in week but in a day.

Spain was now part of the Axis and he must choose. Should he choose Germany, a power that had somehow forgotten its hatred of Godless Bolshevism and had now allied itself with his neighbour, a neighbour that was casting covetous eyes towards his own country and its empire? Or should he ignore the overtures of Berlin and elect to side with a London that, in a desperate gamble, had thrown men and machines into Spain?

But if the British lost, if they were defeated as they had been in France and Norway, then he would have a victorious and even more arrogant Germany on his border.

And then his own life and the life of his nation's neutrality would be measured in hours.

He must choose and choose soon but what if there was a way to delay, even for a short time. What if there was a way to see which of the two contending giants would win? He looked up towards the man who sat with half closed eyes across the desk. 'Mr Ambassador?'

The American's eyes opened, revealing a tired shrewdness that he hoped would aid him.

'Mr Ambassador perhaps you would be kind enough to tell me your government's reply to my proposal.'

The man's accent was patrician and precise. 'Mr Prime Minister I'll cut through a lot of fancy words that you can read later but Washington is not yet ready to accept your proposal to place United States Military assets in the Azores on a permanent basis. I won't bore you with a lot of local politics but my government believes that it does not yet have the support, either at a political, or public level, to undertake such an action.

'However, we have prevailed on our British friends to continue with the attitude that a neutral Portugal is of great use to them. I understand that this particular point is not unknown to you, and that certain plans have been agreed between you and Prime Minister Churchill if it is desired by both parties?'

Salazar nodded. Although they had been allies for centuries, London had not pressed for Lisbon's active participation, and for that he was profoundly grateful.

The drawling voice continued. 'However, my government is prepared to accept your other suggestions of increased diplomatic exchanges and increased commercial investment in your country.' There was a slight pause while a painful breath was drawn. 'And my government accepts your kind offer for a goodwill visit by elements of the United States Navy to Portugal and the Azores.'

This was as much as he could have hoped for and Salazar suppressed a smile and was careful to allow no hint of eagerness to colour his next question. 'When could we expect the pleasure of such a visit?'

'Now, Mr. Prime Minister, or at least within the next few days. My government understands the urgency of the situation and has already issued orders to the Navy Department. As I understand it a cruiser and a few destroyers will dock at Ponta Delgada in the Azores, while a single destroyer will continue on to Lisbon. The ships are already on their way. Both visits will be no more than two weeks, I trust that this is acceptable?'

The rest of the conversation consisted of details and polite conversation and though he gave attention to the American's words, he knew that God had placed a new card in his lap.

He had bought his nation a small amount of time, and in that time he hoped that God or war would show him which path to choose.

But for now, the doubt would remain.

LIGHTS

The man had a salt-burned face and was not at all overawed by the presence of his general.

Jorge had smiled; after all, why should he be overawed, he was a stranger in this man's world, a land animal that knew nothing of the sea.

The American ships were a gift to the sailors of the Republican navy that the tide of war had pushed into Asturias. They loved them as a mother loves her children. Weeks of work had seen them re-engined and their hulls painted a light blue with great gaping shark mouths adorning their bows. But better yet were the great tubes now firmly anchored to their decks.

'Three hundred kilos of explosive, general.' The man was grinning as he patted the fat cylinder. 'And she hits you at eighty kilometres an hour, that's enough to ruin anyone's day!'

Jorge's smile widened. The sailor's enthusiasm was infectious. He truly loved the wooden ships. 'I hear you have named your ships.'

A slight flush rose in the sailor's face but the grin did not fade. 'They are American ships, general, so we gave them American names. La Constitución and La Independencia, our independence and our constitution but still...'

Jorge touched the man's shoulder. 'They are good names... You realise that you are the founder of the Asturian Navy?'

This time the man's face turned red with embarrassment.

Jorge's smile turned into a full laugh. 'Why yes, in years to come, your head will be on postage stamps with a brave motto underneath.'

The man had spluttered at the thought, and then cursed as he realised that what Jorge had said was probably true.

'Well, Captain, I wish you success with your new ships but I have many duties and I can see that the Asturian Navy is in good hands.

The sailor looked shocked at his promotion.

'Wait...I'm a captain? When did that happen?'

Jorge turned back for a second and looked squarely at the man's face and his obvious surprise. 'Just a moment ago; it's a new rule. Sailors whose head will adorn postage stamps must hold at least a captain's rank. Adiós…Captain.'

It was a small moment of humour in a world that was growing ever grimmer and ever more perilous.

When he returned to his headquarters a stern-faced O'Neil was waiting for him, blue eyes shining with a madness only just held in check.

'Roncesvalles has fallen.'

Jorge sighed, he knew that this day would come but still he had hoped some miracle would intervene. 'The garrison?'

'Dead to the last man.'

'And are we ready, Hugh?'

Hugh O'Neil was not a man given to wild gestures, or eloquence so only a shrug of his shoulders accompanied his reply. 'As ready as we can be. Our people will fight, my General. They are weary and sick but they will fight for what we have gained.'

It was enough. Asturias may burn, that could not be helped, but with luck the light from the flames would blind the Fascists. It was enough, it would have to be enough, for there was one certainty.

It would be a long war.

Benjamin Fordson had enjoyed his time in Lisbon. He had visited the churches and gazed in wonder at the gilt and the gold. He had walked the sunlit streets that led to shade-splashed squares and saw with adolescent longing the beautiful women who paraded with artful indifference under the leafy trees. He was a long way from North Georgia, its thin poor soil and its thin poor people.

The patriarch of his family had listened to his hopes and his dreams and shook his grey-haired head. 'Never goin' to happen boy, not round here anyways. Best you take off and take your dreams with you.'

And so he had left; left with a little under fourteen dollars, a spare shirt and a small carving that his grandfather had made.

Many miles and many days later had seen him enter a Navy recruiting office and tell of his dreams of becoming a doctor. The Navy had wrapped its arms around him and, wonder of wonders, had listened to him…after its own fashion and after its own customs.

And after his fashion he had risen, risen to the dizzy height of Pharmacist's mate…third class.

To the ship's crew of the U.S.S Benson, he was "Doc', and it was to him they came to heal their bruises, and to bind their wounds. Though at the moment, the binding of wounds was taking second place to the handing out of headache pills to the long line of sorry looking individuals lined up outside his door. Last night had been the Benson's final day in Lisbon and there were other attractions in the capital besides churches and shady squares.

It seemed as if most of the crew had taken their captain's injunction to *cement the relationship between our two nations* with great enthusiasm and Ben hoped that they would be near a real doctor long before the first symptoms of that enthusiasm began to show. For now, all he could do was listen to the chorus of groans and boasts and hand out aspirin and water, while the banks of the Tagus slipped by and his ship slowly followed the outgoing evening tide back to the sea.

At last the final aspirin was swallowed and the last cut painted with Mercurochrome and Ben was left alone with his books and his dreams. His fingers traced the veins and arteries the second-hand text book showed and he tried to fix the picture in his mind and add it to the growing store of knowledge that would point him along the path to adding the coveted title of doctor to his name.

The Benson heaved as she crossed the bar and the first true Atlantic roller hit her. Ben decided that a day staring into bloodshot eyes was best ended by a turn on the deck. It took only a few moments to ascend from his fume-filled office to the fresher, salt-laden air of the ship's stern where the lights of Lisbon were now no more than a diffuse and fading glow on the horizon.

He sucked in the evening air, feeling it purge from his lungs of the smell of stale vomit and fresh antiseptic while his mind wandered away from the wide horizons which surrounded him to the narrow confines of the valley which had formed his early life. Whatever happened from now on, whatever fate threw at him, he knew that he was not the raw and callow youth who had strode half hopeful and half frightened down the single dirt road leading to the outside world.

The Navy had changed him, and only time would show if that change would open the door to the room where his dreams lay waiting.

The dusk had almost enfolded his ship now and only the last few glimmers of a vanishing land threw their light on the American destroyer. If asked Ben would have said that that his ship was alone, invisible and lost in the night. He was wrong.

Very wrong, for there were others that shared the sea with his ship that night and other eyes that saw the outline of his ship painted against the distant brilliance of a still peaceful land.

And there were other hands that night, hands that moved with purpose and time-honed skill. And move they did, cast steel wheels were turned and power surged along lengths of shielded wire. Water tight doors opened and a torpedo surged forward.

The bow section of the Benson vanished in a cloud of flame and splinters and the destroyer staggered under the blow.

As Ben picked himself up, he knew that whatever the cause of the explosion his place was where cries of alarm were mutating into cries of pain. A short detour to pick up a satchel of bandages and splints and then a dead run towards the now sloping bow, or what was left of it. Ben truly earned his title, 'Doc' that night, though, for the rest of his long life, the men he could not save haunted his dreams. Long after a grateful nation had given him his medical degree, long after he had delivered countless babies, set thousands of broken limbs, that night stayed with him.

He ignored the frantic men who laboured with untouched bodies to keep their ship afloat, He never heard the orders that allowed his ship to summon help and begin the slow and painful journey back to the glaring lights of Lisbon. Blood was his only guide now; the blood that seeped and could be safely ignored for now gauged against the blood that spurted in dying spasms and must be treated before life left with its last pulse, and against the blood that lay unmoving as silent testament and could be ignored for ever.

Afterwards, long afterwards, they gave Ben medals and praise for his work that night but as help sped from a sleep-deprived Lisbon, the world lurched and changed anew.

The report made grim reading and both men sat staring at the folder without wishing to touch it further.

Cordell Hull broke the silence. 'Twenty-seven dead, Mr President; thirty-four wounded, her whole bow blown off. It's a miracle that she survived at all.'

Roosevelt drew angrily on his red-tipped cigarette as he replied. 'Which wasn't the intention at all.'

'No Mr President. The attack on the Benson was a signal, both to us and the Portuguese.'

'Keep off the grass.'

'Yes, sir. We signal our concern over Germany's invasion of Spain by sending a squadron to the Azores and the Benson to Lisbon, and the response is an attack on one of our ships.'

A second cigarette was screwed into the holder. 'Are you sure this wasn't the British,' Roosevelt asked. 'They could have set this up just to draw us into war. The German Foreign Ministry has denied any involvement and hinted that *other powers* may have committed this outrage.'

'I don't think that's very likely, Mr President. London's efforts seem to be focused on keeping Lisbon out of the war, or at least stopping them making any sudden moves. They know that the Portuguese armed forces would need a massive amount of help just to survive and they are already stretched with their commitments in Asturias, Greece and the Middle East. Attacking one of our ships and risking Portugal entering the war, or worse Lisbon finding out that the Royal Navy were the culprits and entering the war on the Axis side just isn't in their interests.'

Hull gave a wry laugh. 'Besides which, Mr President can you imagine our response if we found it was a British Submarine. Why even we might join the Axis! No, Mr President. The attack on the Benson was carried out by a German submarine. It wasn't an accident; it wasn't a mistake; it was a deliberate act designed to frighten us and to show us that the Nazis consider Europe their home turf upon which they will tolerate no interference from us. Berlin can deny all they want to but that is what it is. They know this and so do we. Your speech after the sinking of that aid ship was considered a declaration of war by Herr Hitler and he has acted accordingly. The question is, Mr President, just what are we going to do now? How much further can we be pushed before an actual shooting war starts?'

A strained, smoke-stained grin appeared on Roosevelt's face.

'Starts? Mr Secretary, the destroyers escorting our convoys drop plenty of depth charges. They don't hit anything that we know of but, much as I hate to admit it, Hitler is right. Shots have been fired on both sides and effectively we are at war right now.

'My problem is that the American public don't know it. Oh, I got a flood of letters over that aid ship and I'm getting more each day over the Benson but the plain fact is the American people may be getting a little sore over this sort of thing but they're not ready for outright war just yet. Oh, there's a good deal of sympathy for the British and the Asturians are loved simply because they are the underdogs. Hell, we may even see a few pro-Russia groups spring up if the Russians enter the war. But real, honest to God war? I'm not certain that this nation is ready to face that prospect, and until they do, I'm fighting with one hand behind my back.

'Well, even with one hand tied down, I'm not going to let that two-bit hoodlum go around killing Americans without a response. Firstly, I want those Marines we are sending to Iceland given maximum coverage once they're ashore. I want them on every front page in the country, centre stage on every news reel. The Nazis may hide what they're doing but I want what we do to be out in the open.

'Sound out Congress, find out how much resistance there will be to extending lend lease to the Asturians and maybe to Lisbon. And I want the War Department to investigate ordering more National Guard units into Federal service. If there's going to be a shooting war, I want our boys to be as well trained as possible. Get your people to reach out to the newspapers, Mr Secretary; make sure that they tell every newsman they know that the American government isn't pussyfooting around anymore; that there's a limit, and by God we've reached it.'

Hull nodded in agreement. 'I don't think that we'll have too much trouble with the Asturian aid Mr President. They do have popular support here amongst the people, and it would be a brave man who opposed us sending some military equipment...at least in public. And yes, if we do this then I can expect a visit from the German ambassador, but you may safely leave that in my hands, Mr President.

I will have my reply typed up for your approval by the end of the week.

'As for the Portuguese, the British don't want them in the war and at this stage I would recommend we take the same stance. We don't gain from the war spreading and frankly neither does Portugal. That said, I've received a full briefing from our ambassador in Lisbon. The attack on the Benson was a fairly blunt message to Prime Minister Salazar that he should cease any and all contact with us. There are rumours floating around Madrid, and Berlin too for that matter, that Franco's price for joining the Axis was Portugal...or at least a large chunk of it.'

Roosevelt shook his head. 'I thought those two guys were the best of friends. Didn't they sign some sort of mutual aid treaty a while back?' Another thought struck him. 'Are the rumours true, Mr Secretary. Will Spain and Germany invade Portugal?'

It was Hull's turn to look doubtful.

'I don't know if the rumours are true, Mr President. I'm having them investigated right now. It may be mere disinformation put out by the British or the Asturians, who by the way have built up an extensive intelligence network; but whatever its source, it seems designed to build on Portuguese fears and force them to keep their distance from Madrid. One thing we do know is that there is pressure from Madrid and Berlin on Salazar to join the Axis. The Benson was a sign of German impatience.'

A dry chuckle came from the other side of the desk. 'A not very subtle sign.'

'No, sir. Not at all.'

There was a small silence while Roosevelt absorbed all that he had been told and then he spoke again. 'The treaty, Mr Secretary. Does it force Portugal to join Spain?'

'No, sir. Only at this stage to consult over common interests. The actual declaration of war is still left in the hands of the Portuguese, though Madrid is saying that the landing of British forces in Spain is a threat to the whole of the peninsula. Lisbon's position, so far, is that the Spanish declaration of war pre-dates the British action and therefore the provisions of the treaty that would be activated in the event of invasion do not apply.

'Of course, even though there are low level contacts between Gijón and the Portuguese government, Lisbon does not recognise the Asturians or the Basques as separate nations so any conflict between them and Madrid is viewed as an internal and purely Spanish matter. It's a fine balancing act, Mr President.

'Salazar is to a large extent caught in a cleft stick. There are some in his country who see Hitler's invasion of Russia as vindication of their belief that Germany is a bastion of anti-communism. On the other hand, there are those who think that Portugal is the next mouthful to go down Berlin's throat and that the country should remain neutral as long as possible and then activate their old treaty with the British. Those people are angered by what they see as an attack in Portuguese territorial waters and they believe the rumours that Franco will be pouring his troops over the border any day now.'

'Quite a mess, Mr Secretary.'

'Yes, sir. We are gently pressuring Lisbon to remain neutral but as you can imagine nerves are a little tight over there.'

Roosevelt suddenly laughed at Hull's facial expression. Few could have read it but he had long since learnt to decipher the subtle signs. 'Out with it, Hull. You have a plan.'

A rueful smile broke out on the diplomat's face. 'The beginning of one, Mr President, the beginning of one formed after some effort on the part of my staff and our ambassador in Lisbon. Mr President, the Portuguese are still anxious for us to extend our naval patrols to cover the Azores and to land large numbers of troops on the island.'

Roosevelt shook his head. 'I will have enough problems with Congress when they find out that I've sent troops to Iceland' he, interrupted. 'If I go back and do the same again, they'll eat me alive.'

'Yes, sir, but we can still show our support and give Salazar some cards to play against those who think Portugal should throw in its lot with Berlin. Best of all, it won't cost us a single cent. We may even make a few dollars out of it.'

A new cigarette was lit and more blue-grey smoke was added to the air. 'You have my full attention, Mr Secretary.'

Mr President, my proposal is this. The Azores still need infrastructure and frankly Salazar still sees them as a bolt hole to run to if Portugal falls. I propose that we send civilian contractors to the islands to build that infrastructure - docks, roads airfields, whatever is required. Further, I propose that the contractors hire from the Navy and the Army whatever equipment they require to build these things, and naturally our armed forces will send people to ensure taxpayers' equipment is not maltreated.'

'So we will have troops on the islands?'

'I can't see how it can be avoided, Mr President,' replied Hull to a grinning Roosevelt, 'and with some persuasion the Navy could, purely as an exercise, deliver everything right up to the shoreline.

'I am also going to propose that the Portuguese pay us in Wolfram, Mr President. In part the whole German invasion of Spain was over their need for the mineral and Portugal has rich deposits. The Nazis have been pressuring them to increase their output and renegotiate their contracts. After some discussion, they have agreed to increase output but sell the increase to us, and any surplus monies left over will add to their dollar reserve, which is also good for us.'

'And a poke in the eye for Hitler,' agreed the President. 'It shows that, Benson or no Benson, we're not backing down.'

'Yes, sir. We aren't shooting but our intention will be plain enough, and the Germans will be hurt by it. They gambled on a quick easy war reopening the routes to the Spanish mines. The swift British response and the unexpected resistance they encountered from the Basques and the Asturians means that they're more dependent than ever on supplies from Portugal...especially if British intelligence is true and they intend to invade Russia.

'We will hurt them, Mr President and we won't fire a shot, and if you agree we can have the first men ashore within weeks.'

'And Salazar is on board with this' asked Roosevelt.

'On a personal level, sir, yes, very much so. The Benson incident, angered him immensely and has failed to intimidate him, though he recognises that for the moment he must continue to have some sort of relationship with Berlin. The beauty of the Azores deal is that he can pass it off as a commercial transaction while still showing the Nazis that he will not give in to pressure. Salazar believes that he can convince enough influential people to allow him to continue with neutrality.'

'To walk along the tightrope with him?'

'Yes, Mr President. An apt analogy.'

Hull hoped that he had made a good case but as he expected Roosevelt's keen mind found a flaw in the idea.

'What if Hitler decides not to accept Salazar's position? What if his forces or Spain's cross the border? What if he uses those naval forces he has assembled at Ferrol to attack the Azores which will have American personnel sitting on them defended only by a few rusty cannons? What then, Mr Secretary? Why they'll be burning me in effigy on every main street in America...you too maybe.'

'Well sir, if Portugal is invaded then all bets are off and Lord only knows what will happen but as for the Azores, then they will not be undefended...if you agree.'

There was a curious lull while Hull looked at Roosevelt to see if he had lit a bright enough flame of curiosity in his President. He waited while the cigarette died and the air cleared a little before continuing.

'Mr President as you know the French exiles who fled to Britain have divided into two groups.'

Roosevelt dredged up the memory of a newspaper article he had read. 'Wasn't there a near riot between the two last month, and a failed assassination attempt?'

'Yes sir. The riot was just outside London but it's an indicator of a deeper problem. One of the groups is led by a Monsieur Mandel, a cabinet member of the last French government. He escaped to England under what can only be described as rather extraordinary circumstances and almost immediately set about supplanting General De Gaulle as the leader of the French exile community.'

There was a dry cough.

'He has been rather successful in that regard.'

'Hence the riots and assassination attempt,' commented Roosevelt equally dryly. 'And how does this affect us?'

'Well Mr President, it seems that the Mandel group has several thousand followers who are former members of the French military who have formed, or perhaps reformed would be a better description, armed groups.'

'Armed?'

'They are armed, trained and equipped by the British, sir. There was some talk of sending them to Spain to link up with the Free French fighting for the Asturians but a lack of shipping and some difficulty over their chain of command meant that they did not go. They have not yet formally joined the British Army. Legally they are still private citizens.' Hull took a deep breath and plunged ahead. 'Monsieur Mandel proposes that his men perform guard duties on the Azores.'

Roosevelt's voice rose a little as he took in Hull's words. 'And this Mandel fellow thinks that we will owe him for protecting us; he thinks to get on our good side. Well, that I can understand but just how do I explain the presence of several thousand armed Frenchmen to the Vichy government?'

Hull plunged on, committed now and reassured that at least his idea had not died an instant death. 'Yes, I think that is the general idea, sir. In all fairness, he did visit here some time back and several of my staff, and Mr Churchill himself, speak very highly of him.'

'And this idea would please the British, Mr Secretary?'

Hull grinned a little. 'I think it would. The British are thinking ahead. One day France will be free and Mandel will have a record unspoiled by any involvement in Vichy politics. He may very well have a significant say in what direction his country takes in the future. They may be right, Mr President, and this way we can try him out too: see what sort of a man he is without committing ourselves. He has extended his hand, sir. We could take it without any promises, and as for the French government, the presence of a few thousand private French individuals on the sovereign land of a foreign power is hardly our concern now is it?'

Roosevelt heard the words and looked again at the folder. So many dead, and there would be more, he was certain. The very best he could do was delay the evil day and pray that somehow they could draw back from the brink. He drew a long breath. Prayer was one thing but standing still only gave others the initiative. He must respond to the attack on the Benson and hope the response was enough. A miracle was unlikely but a plan had been laid before him.

He pushed a new cigarette into the amber holder. 'Tell me about Mandel. What kind of man is he, and how much control does Churchill have over him?'

NOOSE

Her way led west. She was imperial might, potent and dominating.

She led her consorts as was her duty and her right. Her way led through the narrow ways that opened into the deep waters. There they would prey upon the unwary and the undefended. There she would extend her might and her imperium. Not for her own glory but for duty and for service. Those were watchwords carved deep into her throne.

Her duty was a bridle and a sure path upon which to walk. Not for her idle boastings and empty chatter. Duty and service would look askance at such things. Her nation was at war and she had been built to serve.

She was Bismarck.

She was duty and she was service.

She was Bismarck.

She was Queen.

Four hundred years.

The Gotland was a Swedish cruiser and heir to four hundred years of battle and service. It was not a thing to lightly discard, and she had the voices of a hundred ancestors behind her. Ancestors that had sailed and cursed and wept and died for her own true land. It was not a thing to lightly discard.

The flotilla in front of her was majestic; each ship had a savage beauty which she knew was lacking in her own compromised lines. Yet the blood of long ships ran through her and she would not fear.

Her voice was gruff and uncompromising. 'Keep off, come no closer! Stay from my shores, lest you come to harm.'

The reply was surprisingly gentle. 'Do not fear. I seek no quarrel with you today; guard your shores as best you may.'

The Gotland's answer was still gruff and still uncompromising. 'They are mine to guard, mine and my sharp-toothed sisters. Come no closer, lest you feel our bite.'

The Bismarck sailed on, her whispering voice trailing behind her. 'I am Queen here, crowned by right. My majesty is paramount. Guard your shores with what little misshapen power you can summon and remember that before me you are but dust.

'All that I survey is mine if I choose to reach out my hand, yet I seek no quarrel, I seek no argument. You have your duty, even as I have mine and today, we meet not in war but in amity. But always remember that I, and I alone am queen.'

The voice was fading now. 'Farewell Gotland. You do your service honour. Guard your shores well until I return to reclaim my throne.'

And then she was gone leaving the Gotland alone with a single thought running through her.

The Bismarck was Queen, that was true. But death comes to all.

Even queens.

'A little over, I think.'

The voice of the fire controller was heard by her guns and they lowered themselves a few fractions of an inch and spoke again in smoke and flames. Eight fifteen-inch shells left her body and flew towards the distant land.

The enemy were attempting to use a road which ran a little inland from the sea. She had closed in the fading light of day to discourage such foolishness.

One more salvo and she pointed hers bows out to sea, content that the road would not be considered again...at least for a while. She had done her duty, she had escorted an army, she had fought off attackers and hopefully now destroyed a road and possibly a few trucks. It was time to go home.

And then as the last of the light vanished, she felt it.

A long mournful cry.

It was not a cry for help but one of pain.

And there was anger there, and a wish for revenge.

And then there was more pain, a surging wave of pain that rolled from north to south and rebounded from the receding shore.

And then nothing.

No voice.

No pain.

Nothing.

She knew then that the Renown had died.

It was full night now and the cold Atlantic air had sucked the last of the heat from her scorched guns.

She'd had the advantage of the fading light; when her adversaries appeared on the horizon, they were silhouetted against the light while she was wrapped in darkness. The exchange was brief, no more than a dozen rounds, and then the sky had lit up with flame and burning.

She was the victor, she was still Queen, her imperium was still whole.

And yet she was not alone, her adversary had consorts. She had killed before they could intervene but now they shadowed her.

Alert.

Silent.

Malevolent.

She could feel the wash of their radar, cold and unwelcome.

She'd sent her consort to chase these impudent spies away and the night was once more rent with flame but they kept returning; always they returned.

No word from them did she hear. Silence was their message. 'You will die,' the silence said. 'Die, die, die.'

Each sweep of the beam brought the same message, a message she refused to acknowledge. She thrashed through the sea changing course at regular intervals, lulling her silent shadows into peaceful acceptance until with a burst she sped away. The radar gave out a last fading touch and then she was gone...lost in the night, lost in the heaving waves.

She was Bismarck.

And her reign had just begun.

A sister had died. She had lost so many sisters over the years; dear friends who had served a common cause; all had vanished behind the black wave that gripped even the proudest, even the strongest.

Her blood debt was growing. Each loss was a voice that was stilled for ever, yet each loss still cried out for revenge.

She had left the Foxhound behind. This was a task for armour and might, not speed and dash. She turned North, vanishing into the cold burning fog, calling out across the waves to others who had joined the hunt.

The coast was far behind her now, her course fixed and steady, her orders clear.

It was time to speak and her voice was heard by all. 'My sister has been killed; killed by those who would usurp my throne; killed by those who have no right to sail these seas. She is dead, and for her sake and the sake of all I am sworn to protect, her killers must die. I look to you all to aid me in my task.

'Rivets must hold all the tighter, boilers must burn all the brighter.

'I must see further, travel faster this day and for many others. And when the day comes, as surely it must come, when I meet my sister's killers, then I must hit harder and hit faster until my sister is avenged. Will you do all that you may, will you allow me to do my duty?'

There was a pause and then a ragged chorus of cheers from every part of her, led as she had half expected by her children.

'We get to play again?' they asked.

'Possibly,' She replied, knowing that this might well be a long-range fight. 'I make no promises though.'

Her caution did little to dampen their excitement, and they whispered amongst themselves in a flurry of hopes and muted laughter.

And so she sailed through the fog, remembering her sister and praying that her enemy would be found.

She was the Hood. And she would have her revenge.

Ships, the sea was full of ships.

Panicked ships, frightened ships, ships that pushed forth black smoke and hurried sparks from weather-stained stacks. Every point of the compass showed a blunt bow pushing through wind-whipped waves determined to leave this cursed sea.

For the wolves had arrived.

It was bravely done.

The two corvettes had stood forth, teeth bared and pitiful guns firing impotently. They could not run and elected to buy precious minutes with their lives. She could admire their devotion but her duty was plain and they quickly died. Her big guns remained silent while her smaller guns spoke with precise words of extinction.

And then the killing began.

Grain ships.

Tankers.

Ships of every type.

She took no pleasure in the deaths. There was little glory and less honour in destroying these ships that could not fight and could not match her in speed. But it was her duty as Queen, and the burnings witnessed her sway over these lands.

She called her consort to her side and they left the smoke-stained skies and the floating wreckage of undelivered cargo. It was time to return, to pick up a few last victims, and then tie up secure and warm with the knowledge that the flag of her cause flew a little higher and a little prouder.

She swung her bow round with regal and potent grace.

Home.

She was going home.

They had been warned.

They knew that there was a chance but it was a big ocean and even a convoy was but a small speck on its rolling fields.

But the Gods of war had laughed at their hopes.

She had heard them. She had heard them conquer their fear. Heard them summon up their blood and their last ounces of steam. She had heard their challenges and their war cries.

And she had heard their deaths.

She said nothing, for what could mere words do but sully their sacrifice?

But the sacrifice had not been in vain.

Delicate wires strung across her had plucked the Corvettes' last words from the air.

Now she knew where her enemies lay.

Now she had a name.

Now she had a position.

The Hood sliced through the waves and on the horizon she saw friendly smoke. Her sisters had arrived.

What in God's name was he doing here?

It wasn't the first time that he had asked the question but he had never yet found an answer that satisfied him. He had a wife and baby girl back home in Boston, a wife and child that he hadn't seen in months. There were days, and this was one of them, when he wondered if he would ever see them again. Certainly, there were an awful lot of angry German gunners down there that were doing their best to make sure that his young wife would become a young widow.

'Perhaps if I told them that I'm an American?'

He shouted the words against the noise of the straining engines as the pilot wrenched the Catalina round in a tight turn that had as its focus the angry mountains that floated below.

'I don't think they're in any mood to listen old chap, besides…'

The sentence was never completed. The captain had a few last seconds in which to view the shattered windscreen and the jagged shard of steel that was allowing spurts of blood to pulse out of his chest. And then he died.

The ships below had hit them, killing both the pilot and the port engine.

He had no time to mourn, nor even the ability to do so. Instead weeks of intense training took over. His hands moved with practised skill, doing all they could to keep the wounded flying-boat in the air and away from the two ships, who had vanished from sight.

A tap on his shoulder broke his concentration and revealed a worried looking radio operator. Speech was impossible in the wind-filled cockpit and the conversation was conducted via a blood splattered note book. He was given a course to steer and assured that the Bismarck's last position had been sent.

Gently he turned his wounded craft around, praying that the compass with its shattered glass was telling the truth when it told him that its arm pointed home.

It was a long way home, and longer still to a child's room in Boston but now he never doubted that they would see both.

He glanced over at the slumped corpse. They had found the Bismarck and her companion but for some the price had been high and for them there could only be a melancholy homecoming.

He stood as he had stood so many times at the despatch box, thumbs tucked into waistcoat pockets, jaw set and eyes turning as he faced the house. Parliament had been restive recently; a stalemate in Greece; a perilous financial situation; increasing losses in the Atlantic; and a British army scraped together and flung onto the shores of the Spanish peninsula.

The murmurs had been growing and it was time to quash them lest they grew too loud.

As arranged, a tame backbencher asked just the right question and the usual babel of voices died and stilled as he began to speak. He thanked the M.P using the tone of voice of a man who had not been expecting the question and had not spent the previous night rehearsing his speech.

'The honourable member has touched upon a great and, if I may say so, most appropriate question, for it touches most warmly upon our conduct in this world-wide calamity which has reached into the homes of us all. I would ask therefore for this house to consider what is our purpose in waging this war.

'Firstly, it is to defend these islands and their peoples no matter what the cost may be.

'Secondly, linked in unshakable bonds, there is an empire, built up, painful step by painful step, over the centuries. This too must be guarded against the depredations of odious avarice.

'But in addition to these grave responsibilities there is another purpose, equally great, equally grave. We must for our own safety and our own security, protect those other nations, those other peoples who have had peace snatched from them. It is the heaviest burden that we as a free people have ever undertaken.

'I need not remind the house that this honourable duty comes at a price, a very great price indeed, and that recently His Majesty accepted, with great courage and calmness, a declaration of war from the Spanish ambassador. History will show I am sure that this will be, if not a turning point in the war, then certainly a grave mistake by the Spanish dictator, who by this action has most certainly sealed his fate.

'Had he but spoken other words and chosen another path, had he urged his countrymen to take up arms against his fellow Fascists then the whole might of these islands and its empire, indeed the whole might of the free world would have stood behind Spain in her struggle. Arms would have been placed in her hands and she would have taken her place of honour in the line of battle. Her past sins, which are many, would have been forgiven and when the happy day of victory arrives, as arrive it must, then the laurels of victory would have crowned her head.

'But none of this will now happen. She has thrown her lot in with the grubby scoundrels who have stained so many other fair lands. Now Spain's people will pay a heavy price for an awful punishment will fall upon them. There are those who say that she signed with a Nazi pistol placed against her head. There are those who say that she had little choice. To those people I would say only this.

'Pistols have been placed against other heads; our own of course, the valiant Greeks who have exhibited a virile and successful resistance to the legions of the new Rome, and most recently the peoples of Northern Spain whose cries of pain have touched the hearts of many. All have taken the hard and narrow path that honour and freedom compel, rather than the wide and treacherous road that leads only to servitude.

'I ask you all, could we stand back while free men and women fight with bare hands against steel and shot; could we remain idle while aged parents and boys torn from the school room stand and stand firm? Could we stay as mere spectators, secure in our island fortress while the horrid flag of Nazism vaunts its evil creed in yet another land? The answer, which came from every corner of this land, from rich and poor, high and low was a most emphatic no.

'This honourable house can therefore most readily understand that his Majesty's government thought it wise to extend the hand of friendship to a people in dire need of our help. Once more the mountains of Spain are echoing to English voices., even as the ancient temples of Greece rejoice that the heirs of ideas first spoken within their columns march in high accord with the sons of those heroes of ancient times. The enemy has hit the Asturians hard; no man can say otherwise; yet they cannot expect to hit without being hit back, and we intend with every week that passes to hit harder.

'This is our aim and our mission, and from it we will not deviate or swerve, however grievous the cost, because we know that out of this time of trial and tribulation will be born a new freedom for all mankind.'

He paused, and then, seeing order papers waved and hearing the cheers resumed his seat. He had them now, any thoughts of rebellion had died here today, killed by his words, which he noted with a half-smile were being recorded by furiously scribbling journalists.

The debate moved on to other matters. He watched as Ellen Wilkinson, his junior minister for housing, cut an opponent into small quivering lumps with icy disdain and hid a grin as the man sat down, defeated and demoralised. The woman had grown into her role but alas, for all her intelligence and all her passion, there could never be anything other than a temporary wartime truce between them. He liked to think that if he had been brought up in the dank, dark back streets of industrial Manchester, he too would have taken up the same sword as Wilkinson and plunged it into just as many enemies but he had been brought up with vastly different expectations and she would never be more than the price of forming a coalition government.

Still her words had filled the chamber and took his mind off the events of this morning which were worrying enough. The Bismarck was loose in the Atlantic.

A whole grey and troubled morning had been spent at the Admiralty watching nervous men converse in worried tones and smartly dressed women with bright false smiles move tiny counters on vast maps.

The Bismarck had struck and killed the Renown in a duel which lasted no longer than it took a man to eat a good breakfast. And then vanished into the Atlantic, shaking off her pursuers with arrogant ease.

He had paced, knowing he was getting in the way but not caring until a grey-faced Dudley Pound forced him into a chair and spoke to him.

'It's bad news Prime Minister. It appears that the Bismarck and her companion caught an east-bound convoy.'

He'd grunted, determined not to let the news dismay him.

'We lost the escorts, H.M.S Cornflower and H.M.C.S Mont Joli,' continued Pound. 'And most of the convoy, fifteen ships as far as we can tell.'

Fifteen desperately needed ships.

Then another thought had entered his head. 'So far.'

'So far, Prime Minister,' agreed the unhappy admiral. 'We expect more losses as the stragglers are picked off by U-boats.'

'They must be stopped, Admiral. They must be brought to justice.'

'We are trying, Prime Minister. We have every available aircraft out looking for them and of course every possible ship we can spare. And as you can imagine, some we really can't spare.'

Pound walked over to a large scale map.

'They were lucky getting out of the Baltic past our patrols but they can't take the chance that they will have the same luck again, so I doubt that they will try and return to Germany. This, as we feared, is no mere raid, Prime Minister but serves a double purpose The Bismarck will run not for home but for Saint Nazaire in France. There are ample facilities for them there and she will be under the cover of the Luftwaffe. From there she is perfectly positioned to take as many runs into the Atlantic as she wishes and to raid not only our American convoys but to seriously interfere with our aid to Spain.

'My staff estimate that to cover the Biscay convoys alone would need the constant use of at least one Battleship, an aircraft carrier and very probably two or more heavy cruisers as well as additional destroyers. It would be an enormous strain and would expose even more of our ships to attack.'

Churchill realised Pound was laying the way open to a solution, hoping that by explaining the danger he would be able to justify his solution.

'That's what I believe Prime Minister and I have made my dispositions accordingly.' A long wooden pointer swept through the air and touched the glossy map. 'The Hood and Prince of Wales here, Victorious here, Ark Royal here, Revenge detached from convoy duty and King George and Rodney moving north, plus cruisers and destroyer groups at these positions. Whichever course the Bismarck and her companion take they will find the way blocked.'

He had nodded approvingly but saw the danger immediately. 'And if you are wrong admiral...if Herr Hitler has decided to recall his ships back to the Nazi bosom, or if it has been decided to seek out our shipping in the South Atlantic as did the Graf Spee, what then? Such a concentration of power in South America could very well tip the nations there into the Axis camp. A Bismarck moored and supported by a sympathetic Argentina could do immeasurable harm to our interests there.'

Pound had gulped, and the lines deepened on his grey face. 'Naturally I have considered the possibility but if I was in Admiral Raeder's shoes this is what I would do.'

Churchill thrust his fears down. He realised that the man was doing what every naval commander had done since long before the time of Drake and Frobisher; he was trying to outguess his opponent. He had left Pound, praying that the man was right, for if he was not, then the noose drawn so elegantly and confidently on the map would close not on a Nazi neck but on thin air.

And now he sat on the front bench listening to debates, which normally would have had his full attention, while his mind roamed far away, seeing tiny ships ploughing furrows on a vast heaving sea.

He looked up as the door to the chamber was opened and an excited man stood at its threshold waving a sheet of paper. He got up, bowed with deference to the Speaker, and taking the man by the elbow, he guided him to a secluded corner. He was about to question him when the dam which had held back the man's excitement burst. 'It's the Bismarck, Prime Minister. They've found her!'

'All our chicks have returned home.'

The voice was joyous. Obviously, the Ark Royal cherished the elderly craft who crowded her flat deck.

'All our chicks returned home and we got three definite hits on her, three hits, sister, isn't that wonderful?'

It was wonderful, though she still had but little faith in these newly fashioned sisters. As far as she was concerned guns, the bigger the better, were the only sure way to kill. But the Ark Royal and her half-fledged sister had done well, which made what she was about to say all the more difficult.

'Sisters your chicks must fly again. It will be long hours before all is ready, long hours in which only you and those you harbour can harass our enemy.'

There was a long silence and then the Ark Royal's voice was heard again, though this time stripped of every atom of joy. 'It will be as you say. Our chicks will leave us once more but it will be full dark when they return and many will fail to find us but all will fly and all will sink beak and claw blood deep in the hides of our enemies.'

And so it was once more as the sea dragged the sun down from the sky, the Ark Royal and the Victorious sent their charges towards the enemy. Later as night fell, as the stars began to press their cold light upon the waves, she heard the carriers calling their chicks home and she heard cries of joy as their decks were punished by fatigued landings.

And there was another sound also, a sound that tore at her. It was the sternly suppressed sobs from the Victorious mourning the loss of crews who had been taken by the night and would never kiss her deck again. She had claimed the right to report her losses and the right to praise their hardihood and their daring.

The Hood had listened in silence and even her children had stilled their excited chatter as the names floated over the water. And then the young, barely broken voice had vanished, lost in grief.

'That was hard listening sister. You must forgive her, for like me she is new to war.' The Prince of Wales was a scant few miles away, her wash just visible.

'There is nothing to forgive, sister,' the Hood replied. 'She saw her duty plainly and acted as best she might. I could ask for nothing more

136

and, though like you, she has but few sea miles under her keel, she has gained a battle honour that will live for ever.'

'Then tomorrow our turn comes?'

Her sister's voice had a hint of nervousness that the new battleship tried very hard to disguise.

'Tomorrow,' agreed the Hood. 'Tomorrow, when the sun resumes his course, our path will bring us to our enemies and they will die. Their sins are great, too great for them to live, for they have killed those who were under my protection. This cannot be, sister. Together we will paint the sea red with their blood as they fall beneath our guns.

The Hood's voice was calm and very, very certain and her sister took renewed courage from it, allowing the Hood to lead the way out into the Atlantic.

Franz Maikranz had never seen his father drunk but the man had undoubtedly taken far too many glasses of schnapps and they had unhinged the iron gates that held captive memories which he had never shared with his son.

'It was us or them,' he slurred, 'us or them. And they kept coming, and that is why it was so bad. They kept coming, those Tommies and we kept shooting, shooting. We were sick of it. We became murderers of men, not soldiers. We tried everything that we could not to kill them but they kept coming.'

Franz was a little shocked. Was this why his father was so adamant that he stay a civilian? Was this the cause of so much argument between them? Could he not see that war had changed, that trenches were yesterday's war, and had he not told Franz's own mother that this ship was a floating fortress impregnable and invulnerable?

His father began to tell a tale of sparing a British Tommy who had tried to rescue his friend from the barbed wire but his voice gave out mid-sentence and Franz was never sure if the story ended because of a surfeit of emotion or of schnapps.

He had gently deposited his father back home to a disapproving mother and left to join his ship. He had understood his father a little better now but there could never be a meeting of minds. And besides time had proven his father wrong. They had slipped out of the Baltic with ease, evading the clumsy British patrols and then the fun had begun.

They had been surprised by a British patrol which consisted of a battlecruiser and two cruisers but he was not afraid, knowing that German might and German steel were invincible. The battle had lasted less than an hour and at the end of it the battlecruiser was no more than a column of smoke on the horizon.

And still they were fortune's favourite; the British cruisers' grip had faltered and once more they were free to roam and kill. And kill they had; two pitiful corvettes and merchantmen without number had fallen before the guns of the Bismarck and the Prinz Eugen and they had driven off an intrusive aircraft.

It was obvious to Franz that the Gods of war had decided to smile upon the Führer and that he was right to bestow his devotion upon a man who was leading Germany to victory. And now after pushing far into the Atlantic they had turned east, towards a new home on the French coast.

But first they must brush aside these antique aircraft which were apparently all that the British had left to throw at them. He watched as the ponderous biplanes clung to the waves while the flak from his ship danced around them. They were slow, so very slow but, just like the Tommies in his father's tale, they kept coming, and at last, when it seemed as if this was no more than a practice drill, they released their torpedoes which ran towards the Bismarck leaving bubbling tracks in their wake.

The Bismarck turned, seeking to evade the attack but could not evade every torpedo and Franz felt his ship shudder as the enemy ran for home, still pursued by angry balls of flame. Then the reassuring voice of the captain was heard telling them that the damage was slight and that soon they would be safe, soon the Luftwaffe would arrive.

The voice was interrupted by the air raid alarm sounding once more and once more the guns of his ship opened fire at a second wave of aircraft which surrounded them with dogged enmity.

Again the Bismarck turned away from the livid, hateful tracks which sought her from every angle but her turn only opened her flank to two more of the phosphorescent tracks which leapt upon her with obvious glee and exploded with suicidal force.

Franz waited to hear his captains voice once more but the speaker remained oddly silent.

Worryingly, oddly silent.

There was more to being a Queen than she had thought.

Grand words to neutral warships were fine and an imperial march through newly conquered waves was another. Killing the enemy when he was alone and unsupported was a necessary part of gaining her ascendency and though distasteful was carried out without passion and with the knowledge that this was her duty. But this constant harassment was wearing her down; her enemies were not content to admit her reign and were gnawing at her even as she sped east.

And they were hurting her.

Already she plunged a little deeper into the ocean, a gaping hole in her side hastily walled off, a few of her boilers now either cold and silent or burned with steam and oil that she hoped were not infected with salt water. She had slowed a little and now her path was marked by the rainbow colours of leaking oil. She was being challenged by those who should be kneeling before her and the very thought of that defiance made her shake with anger.

She spoke again to the turbine which had ceased to turn but only received salt encrusted whimpers in reply.

Still she had faith in her crew; they would make her well again; they would purge the salt from her bunkers and her steam lines; they would take her home.

She steered east, knowing that far to the north the peaceful coast of Ireland would soon begin to slip by; knowing that the night shielded her; knowing that tomorrow her first journey; her first voyage would be over.

Her reverie was interrupted by the urgent voice of the sound locators. 'High speed propellers to the north; many high-speed propellers on a converging course.'

She hesitated. If they were destroyers or better yet corvettes then perhaps she could fight her way through but what if there were many destroyers, what if those sounds were cruisers or even battleships?

She could not take the risk, could not wait until the sound locators were able to tell her for sure what lay to the north, so she made her course a little more southerly, running from the sounds of water being thrust backwards by finely crafted phosphor bronze.

But there was another sound at sea that night, a sound that no cunning device could detect, a sound only the Hood and her sisters could hear.

It was the sound of a noose being drawn tight.

THE QUEENS

She recognised the touch. It was light, just a feathers breath, but it was a kiss that she would, if asked, have avoided. It was the first fleeting finger of enemy radar.

She turned away from its embrace, seeking anonymity in the night-shrouded, white-capped waves.

Another touch, another finger, another turn, another run for home. She left her track upon the water, livid and traitorous for all to see.

Another turn, and this time a turn that gave her sight of two great shapes on the dawning horizon.

Another turn now, retracing her steps, calling her consort ever closer.

Once more the fingers caressed with malevolent intent and then gripped with shocking suddenness.

The noose had closed.

It was not full dark any more, nor yet full light. Instead the new day seemed hesitant, unwilling to leave the no man's land that lay between. Franz yawned. Sleep had eluded him, laughing at his attempts to rest. Instead it had sent images into his head. Terrible images, images of him firing his flak gun until the barrel grew hot and hotter still. While his father's words about the steadfast advance of those lost Tommies echoed in his head.

Like those half-forgotten battalions the venerable biplanes had kept advancing, eluding the grasping waves but not the red tracers that fled from his gun.

He had watched one aircraft which was little more than sheets of yellow flame fly on and on until he could see the pilot's face, his mouth open in rage or pain until he released his torpedo and the sea extinguished both the flames and his life. He knew now why his father's dreams were haunted, why his father had fought so hard to keep him away from danger.

But it was too late, the speakers crackled and then the voice spoke. It spoke of duty and sacrifice, of the Fatherland and the Führer, of glory and honour in the face of overwhelming odds.

It spoke of many things.

But it never spoke of hope.

It was a slow drawling voice that was passed along the wave tops. It held scents of new mown hay, small towns that huddled along a flat fog-ridden shore and sturdy farmers who lived in the Fenlands. It was a familiar voice, one she had heard many times over the years. 'I reckon we got them certain sure, sister. Two of 'em side by side, tryin' to sneak off they is but we got 'em good this time. They 'aint a goin' to get away from us, I promise you that.'

There was a startled gasp from the Prince of Wales and a happy laugh from the Hood at the slow rustic accent of the Norfolk. She knew that though the words were slow her guns were quick.

'They be tryin' to slip between us I reckon.,' added the cruiser, 'I got old Suffolk here now and a few o' them destroyers just waitin' to hear the word, sister.'

The Hood laughed again and gave the orders that would see the Norfolk's group begin to edge towards the enemy while she and her sister ran towards the homely voice. They would hammer the enemy on the anvil of that voice.

The images came as a shock, a frightening disturbing image.

Her back was broken. Flame ran riot through broken bulkheads and smashed frames. As a final despairing effort, she flung her last portions of spite towards a gloating enemy and then slipped forever from the sight of man.

The vision shocked her; for a moment she was far to the north fighting the same enemy amongst the tumbling bergs where the whales gambolled and played. She had lost the fight, lost it before the fight had fairly begun.

But the vision was wrong, a distortion of reality, of what was, and what she could see before her. In her vision she was old and she was tired, dragging a worn body into battle because honour and duty compelled her. But that was not her, that creaking body in the vision was not her, not the one she knew and felt. She was the Hood, and the Hood newly fashioned and potent. She was a killer of ships yesterday and today. Of that much she was certain.

She rejected the vision and it fell from her like an autumn leaf stripped from the tree by a northerly gale. She reached out and touched the minds and souls of her crew.

Determination was there; a task lay ahead of them and come what may all wished to play a part.

Fear was there, suppressed by pride and training but it was a spur and not a bridle, so she had no concerns there.

And in the armoured citadel that towered above her guns there were those emotions too but also a great calm, the helmsman attentive and alert, voices cool and still.

She knew her orders now and was content.

It was time to make her own voice heard and it rang from keel to mainmast, from jack staff to stern post. All heard it, every rivet, every boiler and turbine, every frame and every gun

'All here know me. I am the Hood. I am duty and I am service. I am war and I am death. Together we have walked the sea lanes, fought the enemy, protected the weak. Today I take you all into battle. Today we will sing a new song, a song of triumph. A song which will live for ever.'

Rivets heard her words and tightened against plates that held themselves stiffer, boilers burnt a little brighter as her words carved themselves into every atom of steel and brass.

'Our enemy is mighty, yet we are stronger. For we are the Hood, and we are duty, and we are death. None can withstand us. The sea and the sky will bear witness to our victory.

'After this day has ended ships not yet born will envy us. After this day has ended waves still unformed will cry salt tears that they could not uplift us. And after this day has ended our name and our crew will stand taller still, for we are the Hood and our enemy will hear our song and despair. Do all that you may and we will come safe home.'

There was a silence for a moment and then a ragged chorus of cries and cheers. Even her guns which prided themselves on speaking not often but loudly, gave out gruff words of approval, and then when there was a moment of silence there was a new voice, a voice that surprised her with its maturity. It was the bravest of her children. Of all of them he was loudest and the most playful. 'We promised long ago to protect you. We have kept that promise and would keep it yet. We wish to play our part...and...and...' The newly built dam of maturity broke up under a barrage of giggles from the other four-point fives.

Her children were growing up under the strains of war but a long road lay ahead of them. 'And it is fun to shoot,' she laughed, finishing the sentence for her now stammering child. 'Yes, if all goes well, my children, I will ask you to defend me. Perhaps if you would be kind enough to load with amour piercing and wait until I give the word for you to fire.' The giggles vanished and screams of excited joy replaced them.

She had much to do and the minutes were shortening, so her voice now reached out towards her sisters, touching the heavy cruisers and their attendant destroyers whose smoke was now fast rising up out of the dawning horizon.

'Confound the smaller of our foes,' she ordered. 'Harry and confuse her, give her no peace and no respite, tease and torment her until her only hope is death. Kill her my sisters. Let the sea take her. Pursue her, surround her and extinguish her. This task I leave to you and to you alone I give this honour.'

'Ah, I reckon we can do that sister,' the rolling voice of the Norfolk flowed across the waves. 'Old Suffolk here, she's a goin' to swing round a ways and divide her fire. We'll just keep punching away for a while, then let our destroyers have a little play.' The Norfolk's voice grew graver now, the slow rustic vowels stripped away by the seasoned warrior who lay at her heart. 'Don't worry about us, sister. We have the battle we would wish for. Look to yourself and our new sister, hit hard and hit long and good hunting, my sister, good hunting.'

The Norfolk's voice was drowned out now as her eight-inch guns roared, followed moments later by those of the Suffolk.

The Hood watched as the German cruiser vanished in a forest of tall white spumes of water and then it was her turn.

Her guns began to rise and touch the sun.

Pulver's diesels sucked delicately from the feed lines and gave out not a thunderous roar but a delicate, almost musical hum.

They were not needed yet. Only if a sudden catastrophe were to hit the Hood. Only then would his diesels surge into life and push life giving power into the Hood's bus bars.

And yet Pulver was not content to remain a passive observer while his ship went into battle. He had grown up while serving in the Hood and the thought of her not having every advantage dismayed him.

He thought back to that fateful day when the now lost Renown had hit his beloved ship. The old engineer had been about to induct him in one of mysteries of engineering when his world changed forever. But later, on the long voyage home that skill had begun to flow from an old mind into Pulver's young and admittedly empty mind.

Now he came to a decision, and picked up the phone. Then assuring Stebbings that he would return he left the diesel room.

The Chief Engineer was doubtful. Pulver was a clever man with figures that was true but… Then again, he knew the man who had trained him and that man was no fool. Pulver came highly recommended and he knew the Hood like few others.

'So, you see, sir, it's not my idea at all but I'm sure she can take it.'

Pulver tried to keep the eagerness out of his voice but received only a shake of the head. 'We'll blow a steam line or two and burn out the reduction gears even if we don't.'

It was Pulver's turn to shake his head. 'Sir I saw this ship get rebuilt. I saw every piece of her tested and re-tested by men who knew what they were doing. I won't say it won't hurt her. I don't say we can do it for a long time and I know that we'll be pulling out worn bearings and gears for the rest of this commission but please believe me, the old girl will do as we ask her.'

The doubtful look faded a little.

'I'll consider it Pulver but as the Captain has not asked for any more speed than we're now doing, the question doesn't arise. So, if you would be kind enough to return to your station.'

Pulver did his best not to let his shoulders slump in defeat and turned to go but before he had gone more than a few steps he heard the Chief Engineer speak for the last time. 'But this much I will promise you Lieutenant. If I'm asked to perform such a risky procedure then I know just the man to carry it out!'

It was the best he could hope for and he returned to his station and a relieved Stebbings. They had but a few moments of conversation before a familiar low rumble vibrated through the ship.

The guns of the Hood were rising.

The enemy cruisers had come within range and her guns had sent out warning messages, yet the enemy continued to close and her consort vanished from sight as their shells hissed into the sea.

The voice of the hydrophones was no longer needed for she could see the smoke columns and feel the hate. It was time to decide and time to pay the price of empire.

She ordered her consort to run, to use her speed to seek shelter in the ocean, to leave her to fight the grey-painted monsters that hurried ever near.

She had her honour and her duty still, and they were talismans that had always served her well.

She reached out and touched the minds and souls of her crew. There was fear there but overlaying that was duty and determination. Her crew would stand by her come what may.

And there was realisation, grim realisation that this time was different, this time there were to be no easy kills. But they still had faith, faith in her, faith in what she was and what she symbolised.

And that was enough.

Her voice rang along her decks, through every plate and frame.

'Though green in years I am Queen. And my mark lies upon this sea. I will suffer no dishonour and admit no affront. Those who would spite me must be swept from these seas. I am our nation, I am her spirit and her honour. There is no ship which has been better served, all of you have done your duty and more.

'Soon there will be a last battle and after that all our hurts will be mended and our wounds will be healed. Do your duty, serve my crew well and I promise that all will be well and victory, total victory will be ours.'

Her words were received in silence, for each part of her could see their calling set plainly before them.

She turned her guns towards her enemies and fired.

Her radar's words were sharp and precise; the firing computers took them with joy and translated them into direction and angle, speed and range; and then her forward guns bellowed great sheets of flame and smoke.

A few scant miles away her young sister trembled and then vomited her own hate towards the enemy.

Their shells crossed the miles and erupted into the sea making their intentions plain.

And then came the reply; the waves protesting as the Bismarck's salvo hissed into them. She was hull up on the horizon now and fired again, disappearing for a moment before the wind thinned out the smoke. Again, and again shells crossed in flight as gun fought gun and sharp eyes and cunning computers sought the perfect shot that would kill or cripple. Splinters and sea water lashed her, seeking in vain to pierce her armoured sides.

The Hood led her sister now, her sleeker hull evading the sea's pull, placing her in the seat of honour and of danger.

She fired again and four armour-capped emissaries spiralled their way forward. Three ended their journey in the arms of the sea but one found a new home and nineteen hundred pounds of explosive power hit her enemy. From deep within her bowels this shell had travelled, a special shell, one more rigid, more armoured and forceful, saved along with others equally potent for a day such as this. It bit deeply into the fifty centimetres of finely crafted armour that lay over the very stern of the Bismarck and burst within her.

She had hit her enemy and was filled with joy. She gave a few short words of praise to her guns and they responded only with busy grunts.

But her enemy's reply was not long in coming and a ripple of fire ran down her flanks. The shell plunged down from the sky as just one of the salvos, and though the rest of the salvo harmed only the uncaring sea this last orphan plunged down onto her. It hit the forward four point five, treating its inch of armour plate with contempt, mixing flesh with steel and blood with oil.

A fraction of a second later, still speeding, it hit the forward fresh water trim tank and its fuse functioned exactly as planned, turning eight hundred kilograms of steel and explosives into a swiftly expanding ball of energy that urgently sought release.

The water tank did not even think of resisting. Instead it surrendered, turning its water into steam doing nothing to slow down the blast which thrust up through the wreck of the four point five, flinging its remains disdainfully into the sea.

The shock wave and flames reached the twisted remains of the gun's magazine which added its own power to the carnage twisting frames, blasting a hole through her side and cutting power to 'A' turret.

And then it was over, just a second hand's click divided the shells arrival to the dying echoes of the blast.

'We cannot hear; we cannot move.' The guns voices were an echoing bass that showed no panic at all.

Despite her pain she felt a momentary pride in that lack of panic. 'You must wait for repairs,' she replied. 'I am sure it will not take long.'

There was no reply, and she needed none, for battle was not a time to waste words. She felt around gingerly like a man probing a broken tooth, touching smashed frames and broken bulkheads and then the pain hit her.

This was no mere physical pain. She was a warrior and that pain could wait until battle's end. This was a stabbing sense of utter devastating loss. Her child was gone, the brave one, the one who had promised to protect her that first day and this was gone.

Gone.

Nothing was left but a twisted feed line and a few spluttering cables.

A howl of excruciating grief pulsed from her in a wave of desolation that shocked every plate. And then the grief expanded, supercharged by bitter resolution, amplified by hard acidic anger. She must close with her enemy and close soon, soon while her anger and grief surged within her. She urged her boilers to give their utmost, pleaded with the turbines to turn even faster but to no avail. Her wishes and desires counted for nothing.

Another enemy salvo and another hit. This time the anti-aircraft director room that was perched high up on her after mast was blasted into shards, only adding to the carnage inflicted onto those of her crew who sheltered below.

She was hurting a little more now. Perhaps that vision had been not a bad dream but a prophesy. Long before she could close, long before she could swing her guns in a broadside, she would follow her child, and the great black wave would claim her.

It was then she heard the voice.

Pulver was frightened and there was no point in pretending otherwise. Oh, he could act the part of the attentive officer, he could stand very still and look almost bored but fear was beginning to creep up on him. If he had had a task, any task, then he was sure the fear would fall away but there was no task other than to stay near the quietly throbbing diesels and await orders.

It was the noise that was most difficult to bear. It was difficult to tell the difference between the sound of the Hood's own guns and the booming reverberations from near misses. There had already been one hit; he was sure of that; the sound of screeching metal torn beyond its strength was all too familiar to him and he had placed a hand on the shaking bulkhead and murmured a few reassuring words to the ship he loved.

Still he remained quiet, while his engines remained poised and un-used, and still the icy pebble of fear remained lodged in his throat. And though he felt afraid, he promised himself that he would not let that fear master him; he would not break faith with his ship and the grey-green eyes that waited for him so far away.

For him time was no longer measured with the sweeping hands of the clock but the measured, waiting throbs of his engines, the regular crash of guns and the harsh rumble from the Bismarck's attempts to kill him.

So still did he stand, so intense were his thoughts, that the jarring sound of the telephone startled him.

'Now,' the voice said. 'Report here at once Pulver.'

The walkway swayed a little under his feet from the vibrations of his ship's hurried striding but he paid it no heed as he swiftly made his way to a grim-faced Chief Engineer.

'I may be mad Pulver but I told the Captain your idea and he's agreed to it. God knows, we've little choice. That bastard's beating us to death and the Prince of Wales has troubles of her own. We have to get closer.'

A tremendous crash as one of Bismarck's next salvo struck home added urgency to the man's words. 'Can you do it Pulver, can you give us more speed? I need to get 'A' turret up and running, can you manage on your own?'

Pulver felt the fear drop from him as he nodded and began to give orders. It was then that he reached out and placed a firm, no longer trembling, hand on the ship he loved. 'This is going to hurt old girl, and I'm sorry but it will come out right, I promise.'

All he felt now was a great calmness and a hope that the men of Jarrow had built better than they knew.

She felt the touch, and heard the words. The touch was warm and though the words were odd they were comforting. She felt her lights dim or die altogether as her generators one by one were pulled off line. Released from their burden, her turbines spun a little faster, while the voices of Pulver's diesel generators rose ever higher as uncountable electrons were sucked out of them and sent along a few, a very few, carefully chosen paths.

Parts of her were dark now or glowed only with the blue colour of emergency lights, galleys, berths, pumps and fans, all that was unneeded and unwanted, all were sacrificed for a common cause.

Speed.

And still changes were wrought upon her. Safety valves were tied down and made captive, boilers already burning bright were force fed fuel and air in sickening gulps by over driven pumps until steam already angry was maddened still further.

Nearer and nearer, faster and faster she sped, while turbines screamed and gears grunted.

Hot bearings drank grease pumped into them by men who knew all too well the price of failure, while outside in the cold and the dark her armoured sides ran through the Atlantic.

Nearer and nearer, faster and faster, until the song of protesting machinery rose and rose, until she felt that one more ounce of steam would burst her willing hearts.

Nearer and nearer, while white-faced gauges lied and steam lines bulged.

Nearer and nearer while her propellers fought bubbles of acidic air that picked holes in their bronze smoothness.

Nearer and nearer while she fought the fires that a skidding shell had wrought.

Nearer and nearer, until she felt that touch again and heard the voice once more. 'It's over, old girl. You are where you need to be. Turn now. Turn and face your enemy. Do your best and bring us safe home.'

And then the voice faded and she heard other voices and other orders.

Her enemy's shell had screamed down and cut through the very aft of the Bismarck, ignoring the soft wooden planks and disregarding the thin armour that was all her deck had to offer.

Nineteen hundred pounds of lovingly crafted Scottish steel and explosives ran into the aft machine shop scattering lathes and benches like wheat before the scythe. Still the shell continued, a wave of superheated air crushing all in its path and then the fuse released and the shell exploded.

Only her secondary armour, which lay like a turtle's shell over her vitals, saved her, and in the war of Scottish steel versus German armour, German armour won.

But only just.

Denied its true vocation, the explosion vented most of its anger upwards and a great gout of flame erupted out of her. Her flagstaff, miraculously unhurt rose like a spear and dove into the water in a graceful arc.

But the damage continued and the range finders on turret Dora were never designed to endure such punishment and precision ground glass was reduced to crazed myopic lumps slabs of quartz and silica.

She breathed a sigh of relief as the sounds of destruction ended. She was hurt but she could still fight, her turrets could still shoot, she could still win this battle.

It was many minutes later that she felt the vibrations and felt the sticky dampness. The explosion had released most of its energy back into the open air but enough remained to do more subtle damage. The armoured turtle deck had forbidden entry to the Hood's shell but had been a ready transmitter of the shock wave. The wave, though weakened, had opened the aft most gland valves that held back the sea from the turning shaft that powered the starboard propeller. The patient sea had found a new kingdom and was busy exploring his new domain.

She began to counter-flood, hoping that this act and sealing off her wound would be enough, and that even with a salt-laden turbine and now viciously shaking shaft, there was still a way to defeat her enemies. She roared her anger and her defiance, dividing her hate between the two monsters that dared threaten her but she felt herself slowing as her starboard shaft slowed and then stopped.

At that moment the foremost of the grey painted shapes began to accelerate towards her.

There was steam in every engine room and a great crackling noise as sobbing steam lines and gasping boilers cooled and dried.

Pulver tried not to wince as he looked at the gauges, each needle stubbornly refusing to remove itself from its stop as if protesting at the savage beating it had taken. Only slowly did the needles move from the impossible to the merely improbable.

He offered up a silent prayer and gently stroked the sides of his ship as a man stokes the side of a lathered horse. He had done his part, conquered his fear and now all he had to do was wait.

Wait for his ship to save them all.

Every part of her ached and hurt but now her guns pointed not towards the sun but out over her side, stabbing like accusing fingers. Behind her she could feel her sister hurrying near, her erratic guns mumbling their frustration but turning that irritation into useful packages of fourteen-inch death that were beginning to punish the Bismarck.

The sun, curious to see what was happening in the sea's kingdom pushed aside shielding clouds and shone a white beam on the scene illuminating the ships and turning the wave tops into sparkling white topped flares.

As if this was an awaited signal, the Hood fired her guns in a staggered roar. She could see her enemy now, see the usurper and her duty was plain. She was to become judgement and law, the mouthpiece of slaughtered friends, of orphaned dolls doomed to drift with the tide. Her sister was by her side now and eighteen guns roared against eight.

Yet her curiously slow moving enemy still fired, still seemed eager to kill

A shell plunged into the water scant inches from her side and arrowed into her bulging keel, turning armoured steel and bunkered oil into a red flaming wound.

She screamed with anger and pain and moved still closer, bringing her four point five's into action, urging them to avenge their lost brother, a spur for slim, armour-piercing lances to drill through the upper works of her enemy.

And still her enemy fired and her sister cried out as two shells hit her and her bridge was wrecked. For a moment her guns grew silent but then their mouths spoke roaring words again as she overcame her pain.

Closer, yet closer she moved. She was death now, death made flesh and steel; she was a drawn sword wielded with power and avenging fury.

Another blow now and her radar's voice was silenced as tons of tall steel was axed to her scarred deck.

More and more shells she poured in to her enemy. She could see livid red cracks appear where triumphal flames exulted in their new-found power. And her enemy's guns were silent now, hanging down like a tired man's arms, or blasted upwards, staring blindly and impotently into the sky.

Yet her battle flags still flew and her devoted crew still managed to load and fire a few small guns. That spoke of courage and a willingness to die for a cause.

And die they did as the Hood and her sister swept the Bismarck's deck with yet more death.

And then her guns grew silent, and the smoke from them was grasped by the wind and dispersed across the sea.

Her enemy was low in the water now, her decks crowded with men who had escaped the hot hell that lay inside her.

This was the time, time to ask the question and time to receive the answer that she herself would give.

'My enemy will you surrender. Will you haul down your flags? Will you end this slaughter?'

Despite her pain the Bismarck's reply was level and steady, giving no hint of bitterness. 'I am as my makers made me. I follow my own truth and heed not your law. I fight my battle in the midst of my enemies and have shown them my honour and my mettle.

'Have I not shown that I can kill and wound; have I not shown that I can take blows as well as give them? Would you ask me now after steel has been ripped from me and blood has flown down my sides to lower that which is most precious to me?

'To die in the midst of my enemies is no dishonour. My honour and my flags I will keep.'

It was a just answer and an expected one and her reply was governed by the same customs. 'Then this is where it ends. This is where you must die. I am judgement and your fate is death, for you have killed, and killed in lands that are mine and my sisters. Yet you have fought with honour and for that, and that alone I will give you leave to choose your end. Allow the sea to take you and I will stay my hand for a few moments yet.'

A bitter laugh hit the Hood's battered armour.

'You are too late enemy. Already my keel has been pierced and my valves have surrendered to the sea.'

She was much lower in the water now and her stern was already under siege from the waves.

The Hood watched as men began to jump into the frigid water.

'My crew?' The question was pleading and the Hood knew that like her the Bismarck loved her men.

'All that can be saved, will be saved. I give you my word and the word of my sisters.'

"Thank you enemy, treat them with love as I treated them.'

And then her foe turned over with a great sigh and allowed the sea to claim her and give her rest.

The Hood's battle was over.

And only the Prinz Eugen remained.

She was an exile and an orphan.

She had no home berth, no pier where familiar hands would welcome her.

Yet she was no alien and no outsider. Other hands had extended a welcome and murmured words of comfort. She had other sisters now, far more than before but none bore the same red and white banners of her home land. But no matter what flag, the sea was always the same. To the sea all was eternal and it treated war and peace, enemy and foe with the same cruel indifference.

And the sea carried her this day, this welcome joyful day.

For this day she would avenge.

This day would wipe from her face the insults.

This day she would show that her flag still flew with pride, that though her country shuddered under a thousand whips still she could sting and kill.

She watched with barely contained impatience while the Norfolk and the Suffolk hung onto the flanks of the Prinz Eugen.

And though her enemy's engines strained, and though her bow cut through wave after wave, still she could not outrun the eight inch shells which sought her out with suicidal glee.

Her enemy was burning now, great red flames devouring her and she could feel the fear, that sweet, longed for fear. This was the fear that her own countrymen had felt, the fear that sees death at the hands of savage overwhelming, unrelenting force. Today she was that force, today she too would be savage, overwhelming and unrelenting. For this day she would avenge.

At last a gasping, pain-ridden Norfolk halted her heaving guns and slowed her driving speed. Now it was her turn and the turn of her sister destroyers. They surged in, eager for the kill.

Yet the beast would not die. Feeble spits of defiance she still gave, and her stuttering engines and creaking rudder still turned her away from speeding torpedoes.

It was her duty to attack now, and hate and vengeance drove her nearer yet to her enemy. She wanted the enemy to see her banners, to know who was running alongside them.

She gave a sigh of joy as the torpedoes left her and gouged furrowed tracks in the sea, and she watched as they hit and her enemy lurched in pain. She felt no sorrow and no remorse as the flames grew higher and brighter for this was revenge and just reward for exile and loss. Another salvo and more pain and she felt the scales of justice tip a little more, and joy course through her.

A shudder ran through the Prinz Eugen as the sea began to take her rightful prize, vanquishing the flames with an army of Atlantic waves. A last cry of pain and the sea claimed her, leaving only the battered, hard breathing victors.

The drumbeat of her engines played a slower tune now, and the red light of hate was dimmed a little by shades of satisfaction and contentment.

This day she had avenged.

This day she flew her red and white banners high with welcome joy.

She was no alien and no longer an orphan.

She was a Polish destroyer and she had loosened her nations shackles.

SECOND CHANCES

They were alone, tired, hurt and bleeding, tiny flame-stained specks upon a grey sea, panting with exertion, dazed with the realisation that the battle had ended. They huddled together, exchanging exhausted messages of comfort and congratulation. They were the victors and yet had suffered grievous hurt.

They were turning for home, the invasive sea barely kept at bay by pulsing, shrapnel shredded hoses, when they saw the smoke lifting up from the sea's edge.

As one they turned bleeding bodies to face this new threat while depleted destroyers ran forward to probe these intruders.

They returned with newcomers bearing star studded flags.

Wearily the Hood took in the strange lines and the decks crowded with staring eyes.

It was the Texas who spoke first, her drawling voice drifting across the distance.

'Say, you look a little hurt there. Would you allow me the honour of escorting you to my home?'

The Hood gestured tiredly to her battered fleet, panting out her pain. 'I....I have my sisters with me. They are my shield wall. They will protect me, and I have a home, though it is far away.'

The drawling voice was gentle. 'Yet if you would need a friend, I can offer a safe berth, skilled hands and time to rest. There is a land where all this and more can be found. I know it well for it is my land. I can help now. Let my crew give your own much needed ease. Let my escorts seek in the seas for new threats.'

There was no energy left within her to dispute her new-found friend's arguments and soon the sea was full of boats bearing pumps and tools, and men who clambered up her scorched sides bearing gifts.

But though she was weary still she was puzzled. 'Why are you doing this. Are you not at peace? My war is not your war?'

The answer came back swift and strong. 'I've got my reasons friend, good reasons at that. Seems like your war is bleeding into my peace. Looks like one of my sisters got a little hurt a few days ago. Now I haven't rightly fixed in my mind who did the hurting, though I have my suspicions, and if I'm right then I'm ready, willing and able to deal out a little hurting of my own. And when I do friend, there's certain people who are going to be sorry, that's all I can say. In the meantime, helping you seems to be a good way of showing that Uncle Sam 'aint goin' to be trod on without something happenin' in return.

'You understand friend? We was sent out to find you. This 'aint no accident. I was told 'You go find those folks and bring them home, and don't you take no for an answer.'

And so it was that the Hood began her stay in America.

Franz wanted to die, yet life clung to him with obstinate tenacity. The waves picked up the scarred raft and dragged it to the hot blue heavens only to plunge it down to a wet green hell. Heaven then hell, blue, then green. This had been his life for the past three days.

Three days since the Bismarck had rolled over and taken her last journey. Three days of being lost.

At first he was alone but then in a manner which did not seem odd to him the raft became crowded. His mother, weeping silent tears, his father coldly angry, asking him to remember his warnings that war was not a game. His shipmates, torn and bloodied, yet still the same happy, jesting men they were in life. And the Führer, resplendent in his brown uniform, promising a victory which seemed more implausible as the hours passed. He wanted to die, yet it was comforting to know that he would not die alone.

Heaven and hell.

Blue and green.

A single raft.

A single man.

And the hours turned, each one ushering another.

Light and dark.

Until a new day broke the bowl of night.

It was a game the Foxhound had played before.

Her convoy had swung wide and far away into the Atlantic, away from the French airfields that held the hated aircraft; then, when safety beckoned, they slanted south east towards Northern Spain and released their cargo onto hungry wharfs. But now there was a new danger. Ships bearing the flag of Fascist Spain had been joined by smaller, sleeker ships that had slipped unseen into Ferrol and now provoked her.

Feint and parry, parry and feint, the few defending the many, the fast warding the faster.

The old game, the game of warriors, of kill or be killed.

She had not killed that night but she had driven off the attackers and that was enough although now she could hear her charges anxiously calling her and she swung round, pointing her bow south and east.

The air, even in early summer, took a dreadful delight in robbing Jack McIntyre of much needed warmth. He shivered and took a grateful sip of the rapidly cooling cocoa. He had been set high this morning, higher than anyone else, higher even than the captain. 'Aloft with you, McIntyre, the Petty Officer had said. 'Use those young eyes of yours and keep a good look out.'

And so, in the grey half-light of early morning he had climbed the wet steel rungs to the small steel room where he now sat with only an empty mug, a telephone and a powerful pair of binoculars for company.

Though alert Jack was still young enough to dream; perhaps his eyes would see a powerful enemy battle-fleet on the horizon and the Foxhound would spin round, screaming the alert, causing of course the enemy's eventual destruction. The Captain would naturally ascribe this victory to Jack's keen eyes, and Jack could see himself modestly accepting plaudits and awards, perhaps from the king himself. His mother would be pleased, though she would scold him, as mothers had always done, for putting himself in danger.

His fantasy vanished in a cold bath of reality. There would be no enemy battle-fleet; the last had gone down in defeat in these very waters only a few days ago. There would be no flashing guns today. What was more likely was the evil eye of a jutting periscope or the foamy wave of a torpedo boat, and for them he must be on constant guard.

He blinked rapidly and wiped his eyes, then placing them into the soft rubber cups of the binoculars, he swept left to right as he had been taught, concentrating not only far but near.

He saw only the steep sided waves, marching to who knows where, pushed along by a hurrying wind that scattered their tops into white foam. Again, and again he swept. For the next two hours he was the eyes of his ship and over a hundred men depended on him.

There was nothing.

No periscope left a slim wake, no enemy bow broke the eternal symmetry of the waves.

This was his watch and for that two hours he held his shipmates in his hand, dreams and fantasies forgotten.

A last sweep as he heard relieving footsteps on the steel rungs, tired, eyes narrowing as they sought to vanquish the growing glare.

There!

Right before him almost on the horizon was something, something that did not belong, something that was not sea, nor yet an enemy.

He hesitated, his hand hovering over the phone. This could be no more than wreckage, the remains of an ancient tragedy, yet there was something about what he saw that compelled him to report. The Foxhound heeled over, slowing slightly in response to his words, yet never stopping, for in these waters a stopped ship was a dead ship.

Jack was on deck now, his duty over, tired eyes forgotten as his object revealed itself to be a battered raft that lifted and fell in the waves. Its only occupant was a man whose skin was reddened and blasted by sun and salt, and who looked up at the grey cliff of the Foxhound with dim uncomprehending eyes, unheeding of the cries that urged him to scramble up the net that had been flung over her side.

Jack looked into those eyes and knew he must do something. A few hurried words to the deck officer and with a length of rope tied around him he scrambled down the net.

He would have one chance.

And one chance only.

The Führer was screaming at him, arms flung wide, urging him to attack, to gain victory, to free Germany. He tried to summon up the energy. Yet now his father would not let him move but stood in front of the Führer unsmiling and strangely wearing the uniform of a British sailor.

He tried to ask his father why he was wearing an enemy uniform but received no answer. Instead a rope was fastened around him and he felt himself rising, leaving the water-sodden raft. Dully he believed that this was the longed-for death; that he was being pulled up to heaven and there he would meet his shipmates in a final reunion.

He tried to mumble a childhood prayer but his exhausted body closed its eyes and the prayer ended before it had fairly begun. He never noticed the young sailor making a desperate leap for the netting and arriving by his side with water dripping onto the Foxhound's pristine decks. He never noticed the crisp white sheets that enfolded him, nor felt the soothing balms that sought to heal the ravages of sun and salt. He never knew that a debt, decades old, had been paid.

But for Franz Maikranz, though death had touched his sleeve, the war was over.

She growled her impatience at the delay. Her charges were calling her, and this was a land where wolves prowled. Too slow, even for a moment, gave advantage to the sharp-toothed killers and the thought of failing in her duty sent shivers of unease running through her.

Her sisters were few. They had been drawn far away into the hunt for the enemy giants and all had now retreated to lick their wounds and heal their hurts. There were too few sisters and far too many duties.

She was almost alone, only a trawler armed with ancient cannon guarding her flock and though she bore the flag bravely, the killers who roamed these seas would barely pause for laughter before despatching her.

She must return and with speed lest her convoy scatter before the winds and her task end in failure.

Her hearts quickened their beat and once more the white wave appeared at her bow.

She was the Canarias and bore the flag of Spain.

She was Spanish from keel to mainmast, and quivered with anger.

Too late the call had come; too late had she left the Ferrol breakwater; too late had she hurried to the battle only to find wreckage and the smoke of war long gone.

Too late had she come to the aid of an ally.

There was nothing left; a few bodies, a rainbow oil stain and the lingering whispers of defeat. The guns had quietened and words of war and farewell had long since been spoken.

She had circled the scene, powerless to help and then turned, honour unsatisfied, anger coursing through her plates.

There was a debt owed and she was determined that it would be paid.

She turned...and not for home.

He was a captain now, by presidential decree, though if he was honest, he did not feel like a captain, nor look like one. He still had the same blunt nose, broken too many times, the ragged, black, curly hair and the square jaw that badly needed a shave. Only his mother truly adored that face, and though a few women had professed to love it he knew that those words were encouraged more by the money passing into their grasping hands.

But he was a captain, and he did have a ship of his own, one that he loved, a new sleek and fast killer that he lavished care on, and was sure loved him in return.

A washed-out blue covered her, blending smooth lines into the sea, disguising her intent. Two fat tubes jutted from her, eager to spew from their mouths torpedoes that he prayed would run straight and true.

Beside him the other half of the Asturian fleet, equally blue, equally eager lay waiting, a faint grey stain of smoke hanging over her blue steel exhausts.

He waved his hand and the fledgling navy, built in America but proudly wearing new names gently left the docks and pointed their shark mouths towards the open sea.

He was a captain and had a war to win.

No more than two horizons separated the Foxhound's convoy from friendly wharfs.

Attacks had been beaten off, though one of her charges lay low in the water and the great fire-driven column of smoke that rose from her removed any possibility of hiding in the ocean. It did not matter; she had protected and she had shielded. Funeral black smoke had covered her convoy and many an enemy had cursed her name and written it in blood upon their wings.

She gathered up her scattered flock, barking orders, fearing that other eyes would judge her if her charges entered harbour disarrayed and dishevelled, rather than in the serried ranks that would show her prowess and her skill. It was hard work, for the convoy could smell the land and wished only to feel river water under their keels. She growled and snapped, harried and chivvied but at last there was order and her task was nearly done.

It was then that the trawler gave the warning. Far out to the west, she was a lone lookout. A startled cry, cut off after a brief interval, was her only memorial but it was enough.

The Foxhound turned to meet her foe.

On a day like this it was a joy to be a captain. The sun shone and the few clouds gazed down on him with mild condescension. The land slipped by, houses and docks giving way to isolated farmhouse and then bare rocky headlands that grimly resisted the un-sleeping sea.

The welcome convoy was not too far away. In his imagination he could almost see them, long lines of ships that bore guns and bullets, food and clothes; everything his young nation needed to keep them if not safe then free.

The vision died as the radio burst into life and the first panicked ships hurried past him, eager for the safety of land. They told of a Fascist ship that had sprung up out of the morning mist, of gunfire, of a desperate duel that could have only one ending. A half-smoked cigarette was flung into the sea and his left hand pushed the twin throttles forward until steel levers hit steel stops.

He was smiling now as the wind rushed past his face and his engines roared.

The bows of the Constitución and the Independencia lifted as the Asturian navy went to war.

She had moved fast but still she hurt. It was hard to avoid every shell that her enemy flung at her but she still stood between her foe and the precious convoy.

She had growled when she recognised her adversary. This was the ship that had attacked her so long ago.

As before the proud voice had come to her. 'Let me pass little one lest you come to harm as once you did. Let me pass and I promise that I will waste no shells upon you.'

The barking answer was instant. 'Waves will close over my deck before I allow you passage. Once before you attacked when my back was turned. Are you willing to face me now that my guns are ready?'

There was no reply but the Canarias shrouded herself in gun-smoke.

And the battle began. She laid down smoke and hid in it only to burst from it, taunting the Spanish ship and firing her torpedoes at long range. Every second out of the smoke brought danger to her and priceless time for her charges.

Her torpedoes fell to the sea floor one by one but the Canarias's shells fell all around her and once more she was punished and out ranged by the larger ship. There was only one path open to her now; she would ram her adversary with every ounce of steam.

The attack would kill her but cripple the enemy so that the convoy would survive and her honour would remain untarnished.

She turned into her smokescreen and out into the unsullied brightness that lay beyond. Soon she would enter it again and set her course for collision and her steel would immolate itself against the armour of her hated enemy.

It was then that she heard the strange voice.

'Now this is fun. Them waves; why they just couldn't get out of the way quick enough!' She giggled to the sleek blue shape that kept pace with her. 'Hey, sis. 'Ain't this fun? You think them ships was right; that there's trouble ahead?'

Her sister, though born in the same yard, was of a more serious frame of mind; to her speed and dash were merely tools that would enable her to kill with efficiency and minimum danger. Nevertheless, she loved her more frivolous sister and permitted herself a slight smile. 'I aim to find out sister,' she replied. 'Them ships were spooked for sure. Ain't no reason for that 'less there was a little fight'n like they said.'

'Sounds like fun, sis. Hey, looka dat. Ain't that smoke?'

A great bank of black smoke was fast approaching and out of it was emerging a flame ridden shape that gave off waves of grim, pain-filled determination.

'Yeah, you rite. Now don't you be dashin' off some. We take this real slow. Now let me talk to that stranger. Hey, where y'at?'

Disturbingly there was no reply from the stranger and even more disturbingly she noticed that the stranger's forward guns were trained on her and her sister.

'Maybe she don't speak plain English, sis. Maybe she's one o' them German ships we 'bin hearin' about.'

'Hush, sister. Let me try again. I'm sure she's British but she's hurt real bad.'

She spoke a little louder this time, hoping that volume would overcome any difficulties. 'Hey where ya stay at?'

The stranger, despite trailing flames, continued to run at them, seemingly determined to remove them from the waves before returning to whatever task she had been doing before their arrival.

There was panic in her sister's voice now. 'Sis! Tell her that we're friends. She's fix'n to fire!'

'Hey don't shoot. We're Asturian, don't shoot! Look we have the Asturian flag!' She turned broadside on to the onrushing destroyer, and the flag with the yellow cross and red star stood out plainly, stiffening in the diesel-generated wind.

The barking voice held a good deal of pain and a hint of apology. 'I'm sorry. I thought you were German. I could not understand you.'

They were a little hurt by that, though it was possible that the considerable hurt the destroyer had taken had reduced her ability to understand speech. Still it was time for introductions. 'We're the

Constitution and the Independence. Course in Spanish it sounds real fancy but that's who we are, born in the great city of Nyoo Alllyins and built by the great Andrew Higgins his-self.'

'And I am the Foxhound. I was escorting my convoy when I was attacked by a Spanish cruiser, and...' A thought rammed itself forward as the memory returned. 'My convoy, did it survive?'

There was a giggle which did not even attempt to suppress itself. 'Well there's a few o' them that will have a little oil in their bilges tonight, I reckon' that a few o' them just about...'

The sentence was never finished as her sterner sister interrupted. 'Hush, sister. This ain't the time or the place. Can't you see she's half out of her mind with worry, and what if that cruiser decides to take a few pot shots at the roadstead. Why massacre won't be in it and that's a fact.'

She turned her attention from her jesting sister and spoke again to the destroyer. 'Your convoy survived, looks as if you bought them time. Seems to me as if we need to join forces, friend. Seems to me as if we need to show that cruiser, she 'ain't welcome round these parts.'

The Foxhound swallowed her pain and attempted to hide her doubts. 'Can you do this? I...that is...'

The serious voice did not take offence. Others had seen only their small size, never seeing the hearts that beat within them. 'Oh, we pack a wallop, don't you worry none about that. We're eighty-two foot of plain, old fashioned meanness. Any moment now, that there cruiser's goin' to come a lookin' for you. How about you do what you was goin' to do and go right down her throat while me and my sister here, we come in on either side of you and get real close, real fast.

She borrowed a little of her sister's levity and sent a wide grin to the still smouldering destroyer. 'Besides,' she said. 'You think you can stop us? My sister here; she's just itchin' for a fight.'

Her sister agreed. 'Gonna stick my torpedoes so far up her...'

'Time's a 'wastin' friend. You coming?'

Together the three ships turned and entered the black smoke.

To stay or to go?

To wait this side of the smoke screen, or to burst through not knowing where her adversary lay? She had wounded the destroyer, smoke and flames were true evidence of that, and she was but a single destroyer. What further harm could she do? A few more rounds and the matter was settled and then the convoy would be hers, locked in the road-stead, unable to flee.

Yet what if her enemy was waiting, puny guns and dangerous torpedoes poised and waiting? She had heard the taunts, daring her to follow, to enter the oily blackness and those taunts had stung, and stung deep. The indecision gnawed at her until the pendulum of doubt ceased its swing and she surged forward towards the oily smoke, determined to avenge the insults and then feed on the convoy until her guns grew weary.

It was the wrong choice.

While she had hesitated other, quicker minds had met and allied.

At first all seemed well, a high-pitched war growl and a flame splashed bow announced the British destroyer. She could see her enemy's plan, a suicidal rush ending in tangled steel and the end of her mission. She smiled a little, knowing that her guns, large and small, would show the futility of such an act.

A small amount of rudder turned her broadside on to the rushing destroyer and she waited until she was sure that every shot would tell and the seabed would receive only twisted metal.

It was the wrong choice.

Seconds after she had steadied on her new course, two new, widely separated shapes crashed through the thinning smoke. They hugged the waves, their blue painted bodies blending with the sun warmed sea. Only their bows stood out and visible through the broken waves were rows of white painted shark teeth and, most terrifying of all, two red-lined eyes that stared at her with blind visceral hate.

'I'm back, enemy.' The Foxhound's voice was an aggressive howl, filled with pain and vengeance. 'And this time I've brought some friends who are most anxious to meet you.'

A four-point seven-inch shell hit the destroyer and she staggered a little but she did not slacken her pace, nor pause her words. 'Yes enemy, most anxious, and they come bearing gifts; gifts that you will long remember.'

The Canarias tried to track the two smaller shapes but they were moving too fast and too erratically and she could not ignore the destroyer who still lunged at her throat.

She never saw the torpedoes that killed her.

'Reload! Steady now, steady.'

His world had narrowed until he saw only the grey sides of the Canarias. He was under her big guns now and even her smaller guns struggled to hit him.

Two more torpedoes were loaded and time slowed as his engines struggled with the twin tasks of running his ship at full speed and charging the compressor which would allow the French-made weapons to run against his enemy. Slowly, oh so slowly did the needle move but it reached its mark for less than a second before a quick hand slammed down on the release and a thousand pounds of pressure released their eager lances.

A burst of gun fire raced across the cockpit and a hot sliver of metal sliced across his brow. Blood flowed down into his eyes. He cursed and tried to follow the tracks with half-blinded eyes and so never saw the cruiser swing wide to avoid his own thrust and run full tilt into two more torpedoes.

He never knew who fired those torpedoes, whether it was the wounded destroyer or his sister craft, who like him was determined to write the first page in the history of the Asturian Navy.

Ultimately it did not matter, for those two hits marked the end of his enemy as a fighting ship.

They hit her and hit her again until out of ammunition, hurt and exhausted they left her burning and dying.

Later, as he gingerly touched a crude bandage, he reflected that it was indeed a joy to be a captain.

The Hood had lost her sisters as one by one they were called home to repair the rents that a day's battle had delivered upon steel and flesh, and at last only her path led west.

Her new friends had joined forces with her exhausted crew, and with many a cunning device-built walls against a sea angered that she too had not died that day. They pointed her towards the new world, a world without the crash of bombs or the high scream of searching shells. A land of plenty and of that now forgotten virtue…peace.

The Texas had left her at the harbour's edge, pleading duty and assured her with a barely subdued laugh that she would receive a hearty welcome. 'Give my regards to Mother,' she shouted as she and her escorts had turned back towards the rising sun.

The Hood had slowly been pulled to a long-desired wharf and soon forgot the cryptic comment in the noise and bustle of making of making fast. The last of her over-taxed boilers sighed with gratitude as oil ceased to burn and settled into a well-deserved slumber. Her children, exhausted after the battle, ceased their chatter and dozed, dreaming of glory and shrapnel.

Her pain had subsided to a dull ache as night enfolded her in soft warmness but sleep eluded her as scenes from the battle appeared within her. She felt no regret, no remorse over the death of her enemy; there had been no hate, only a task that duty had placed before her.

But there was time now for grieving, a time to mourn the lost. Her child now walked only in her memory, and though another child would take his place that was of little comfort. The night was complete now but still she brooded, wondering if her actions could have been different, if lives could have been saved.

Had she failed?

Were there men now dead who would still live if only she had cut at her enemy deeper?

The voice broke into her thoughts. 'It's always difficult isn't it? After the battle I mean…You don't have a chance to think at the time but after? It's hard, I remember. You're hurting now but it will get better, I promise.'

The darkness was total and she could see nothing but she was still a warrior and issued her challenge.

The reply held gentle warmth with a little hard iron. 'You ask who I am? I was long ago given a name, an honoured name. Then I was given a name in the midst of battle and I have carried it ever since.'

A dry chuckle floated from out of the night. 'Are you confused? Then I will tell you a tale.

'Years ago, before your keel was laid, I was a forest, green and bountiful. Then I was lumber cut and fashioned with skill. I was a warrior, my country's voice, proud and strong. Then I grew weak and feeble but was reborn as an envoy for a land growing in strength and power. For a time, I was nurse to those still green in years. Today I am memory made solid in hemp and tar, oak and iron.

'You ask who I am?

'To the nation I serve I am the Constitution; to my crew I am Old Ironsides; to my daughters who guard our coast I am Mother, and like all mothers give advice and counsel to my children that they take or ignore as the fancy takes them.

'That is who I am, and though you wear the flag of an ancient adversary my daughters tell me that you fought bravely against an enemy of theirs that hides his enmity behind fair words. For their sake then I bid you welcome, though I confess that to see that flag so close is a mite troubling.'

Though the Hood was weary she would not take an insult however mild to her flag. She summoned up the last of her strength and all of her pride. 'I fought the enemies of my country. I fought those who had killed and would kill again. Would you have done less? Though my flag is stained and shredded no one insults it and lives. Those are my words, do not doubt them.'

There was a small hint of apology and old admiration in the reply. 'Easy, child, easy, I didn't mean to rile you none. It's just that seeing you today brought back a lot of memories. I'm more used to seeing that flag attached to ships that were trying to kill me.'

'You fought my flag?'

The chuckle turned into a deep laughter. 'More than a few times child, and I will say they took their medicine without too much crying and wrote their words fair for all to see but like I said that was a long time ago and my daughters, who are not easy to impress, told me a little of what you did. Word of your battle reached me long before you showed up and I readied myself. I heard you mourn, and remembered what it was like for me.

'I too lost men, good men, men whose names are forgotten and lost in my wake. Yet I remember them, the good in them and the bad, and because of that they live. That is how it must be for you. Grieve

170

if you must, mourn if you can but take heart from their loss. Retain their honour, for it will serve you well in the years to come.

'That's my advice to you child. Take the word of an old warrior and let time smooth your path. What's done is done. Ain't no going back.

'I hear you are going to be sitting here a spell. Best take that time to heal; from what my daughters tell me there's work 'a plenty out there for you to do. Ain't no point frettin' now. You just rest...and if you need me, I'm right here.'

The Hood heard the words and took comfort from them and a little of her burden fell away. Her dead would live on. Their faces and their last thoughts were part of her, now and forever, and though lost to the world of men, they still added to what she was and what she would be.

She was the Hood.

She would live again.

Fight again.

Of that she was quite certain.

FICTION FROM APS BOOKS
(www.andrewsparke.com)

Davey J Ashfield: Contracting With The Devil
HR Beasley: *Nothing Left To Hide*
Lee Benson: *So You Want To Own An Art Gallery*
Lee Benson: *Where's Your Art gallery Now?*
Lee Benson: *'Now You're The Artist…Deal With It'*
Nargis Darby: *A Different Shade Of Love*
Jean Harvey: *Pandemic*
Michel Henri: *Mister Penny Whistle*
Michel Henri: *The Death Of The Duchess Of Grasmere*
Michel Henri: *Abducted By Faerie*
Hugh Lupus *An Extra Knot*
Ian Meacheam: *An Inspector Called*
Tony Rowland: *Traitor Lodger German Spy*
Andrew Sparke: *Abuse Cocaine & Soft Furnishings*
Andrew Sparke: *Copper Trance & Motorways*
Phil Thompson: *Momentary Lapses In Concentration*
Paul C. Walsh: *A Place Between The Mountains*
Michael White: *A Life Unfinished*
TF Byrne: *Damage Limitation*